GET BA

BRADLEY

REVENGE HAS NO EXPIRY DATE
AND BRADLEY NEVER FORGIVES.

JAY WORD

JAY WORD

Get Back Bradley

Revenge has no expiry date and Bradley never forgives.

First edition

This book was professionally typeset on Reedsy.
Find out more at reedsy.com

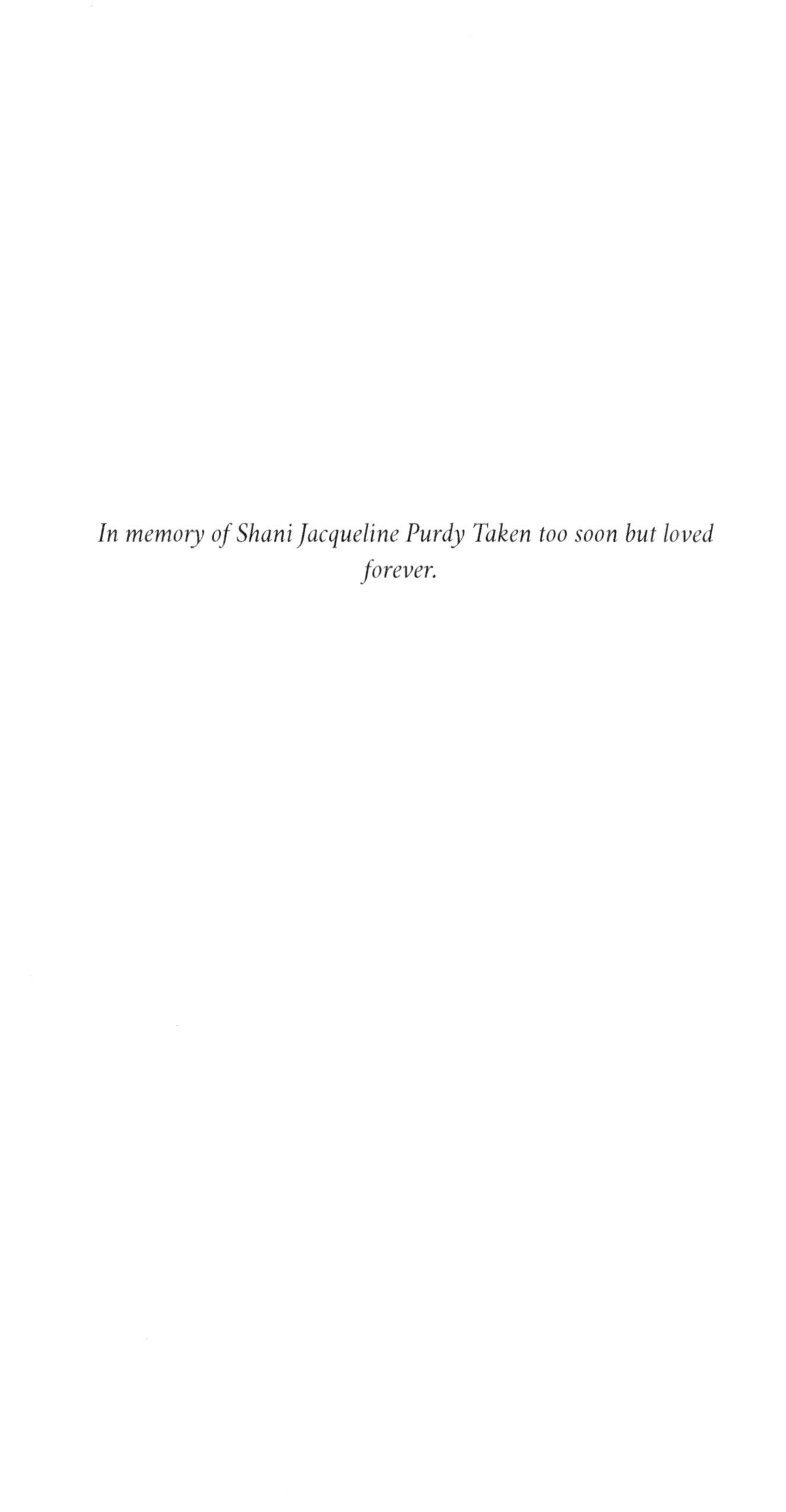

In memory of Shani Jacqueline Purdy Taken too soon but loved forever.

Contents

I

2009

WANT ALL, LOSE ALL

Greed will cost you in the end

BRADLEY

"That boy is dead!" Bradley shouted at his own reflection in his mirrored, floor to ceiling Ikea wardrobe, simultaneously throwing his iPhone 3 across his bedroom. Bradley then punched his fifty inch plasma television which was mounted on the wall, as if it was Joseph's face. Not once or twice, but three times for good measure. He'd just got off the phone to that pussy and he could tell that Joseph had been lying. He just knew it! Who else could it be? Nobody else knew about their hiding place; the brick that they pulled out of the chimney breast wall. It was concealed behind an extravagant, electric fireplace. Nobody knew about that except himself and Joseph but yet two men wearing all black and masked up, had smashed the back door in and robbed them. Well, robbed *him*.

Bradley had watched the violation in real time, on his phone via their security system but because of what they had been guarding, it was not connected to any security company or the police. When that alarm was triggered, it alerted only two people. Bradley and Joseph, who just happened to be on holiday together when it all went down. Bradley hadn't even wanted to go on the stupid holiday. He'd been focused on making money, rather than spending it but there were other concerns that Bradley had raised with Joseph and getting robbed, had been at the top of the list. Now it was looking as though his own boy, his partner, had fucking snaked him.

Joseph had begged and begged about the holiday, even resorting to emotional blackmail; his father had recently died and Joseph *had* actually been looking like shit. Bradley had witnessed his friend break down on many occasions over the past six weeks or so and it had been a while since either of them had used their passports, so in the end Bradley had caved in and agreed to go on a short break with his *friend*. He'd told himself that he was just being paranoid and that there was nothing to worry about because of the alarm and cameras but he would be in for a rude awakening whilst chilling at a beach club in Zante.

On the second day of what should have been a five day holiday, half way through the night when they were more two thousand miles away from home, Bradley saw the act that was going to end up costing lives. He had also seen the guilt in Joseph's eyes - the pussy's face hadn't been able to hide the deception even though, he had definitely been trying to come across as shocked as Bradley. Not a very good actor though, Joseph, Bradley thought to himself. Joseph had set him up. Yes, half of it could have been Joseph's, but he was behind on payments so technically all the coke had belonged to Bradley and Joseph had got some goons to rob him whilst they were away. Bradley could see it on his face, at the club in Zante. He'd seen it on his face, when they had returned on the next available flight back to London.

Bradley had expected Joseph to go with him straight from the airport to their spot, to check the damage and to arrange for the smashed-in back door to be fixed. They had been lucky that it hadn't rained before they'd got back to the UK, but again Joseph had behaved suspect; seemingly unbothered about their predicament. He'd told Bradley that he needed to go and check up on his mum as a priority. Bradley understood that with his father now gone, Joseph was the man of the house, and that he had a duty to care for his mum but they had just been robbed and Joseph was acting like it hadn't happened. They were meant to be on holiday for a few more days anyway, so why did Joseph need to rush home? Why wasn't he mad too? He should've been fired up to ride out with Bradley and find the pussies that had robbed them. Instead Joseph was on some, *I'm twenty-five with two kids now, man ain't on that no more,* bullshit. But he *was* on robbing his main boy it would seem.

The stash house was a private let through some local Asian guy, who had a large property portfolio which covered much more than just their local area; the lads didn't always stash their drugs close to home. They had to move around - Wandsworth, Vauxhall, Streatham - anywhere within the SW postcode, where they didn't have rivals, who'd rob them. And areas where residents were less inclined to report suspicious activities to the police; the police didn't appear, to have been alerted of the break-in whilst they were away and Bradley needed it to stay that way.

Bradley had been worried about being robbed by his rivals but it had been a friend and not an enemy, who'd actually done him over. The two men, never used a house for more than six months at a time and it had been approaching the time to move on but it had been Bradley making all the payments of late - for everything. Now he'd been snaked by the one guy that he'd always thought that he could trust. Vexed was an understatement. Bradley was livid. Well if Joseph thought that he was going to get away with it, he had another think coming, because Bradley Brown did not take being snaked, lightly.

Half a kilo of cocaine had been stolen from their fucking stash house and Joseph was moving shifty, instead of violated. To Bradley, that was a sure sign that Joseph had been behind the violation. Joseph had been Bradley's boy from day one at secondary school. Bradley didn't fuck with many people these days but he'd known Joseph since they were eleven and he'd never have believed that his bro could do this to him. But Joseph had done it and now it was done between the two men. Dead! Just like Joseph would be soon, and he knew exactly what Bradley was like; having been witness to plenty of blood that Bradley had shed, in the past. The days when they were both wild and running with the boys from SUK (Stay Up Krew) named so because they claimed to always stay on top of the leader board, in their attacks against opposing gangs.

The gang claimed to have the most bodies - murder victims - in London, and Bradley would personally affirm that most of those bodies were his. Lives that he had actually taken. Not always alone. Sometimes it had been a joint enterprise. Bradley had stabbed more pussies than he could remember. Joseph had been less active because he was a pussy himself, and because of this very reason, Bradley saw what Joseph had done to him, as an even bigger audacity. Joseph was too shook to try and rob their rivals but he was cool with robbing his friend, his *bro*. They were supposed to be like *family*. They had slept top and tail as kids and their mothers knew each other but Bradley had been betrayed by his own flesh and blood in the past, so he was beginning to feel like a fool, because he had allowed it to happen to him again. This was not how Bradley had expected his week to go. He was literally, foaming at the mouth.

"Fucking wait till I get my hands on that bitch," Bradley screamed at his own reflection again, then punched the mirror hard, shattering it and cutting himself in the process. As spittle and blood ran down the damaged furniture, there was only one thing that Bradley was sure about, and that was that Joseph fucking Aku was going to wish that he'd never fucking met him.

Alligator lay egg, but he's not a fowl.

Joseph had played the part of a loyal soldier for years but he'd shown his true colours now and Bradley would not make the mistake of trusting anybody, ever again. He was going to treat everyone as though they were an alligator from there onwards because he knew that anybody was capable of doing anything. He'd fallen victim to snakes, too many times in his twenty five years of life. Including his own family. His blood. But everyone would get what was coming to them eventually. It was holding onto this knowledge, that got Bradley through each day.

He hadn't forgotten about, any of the treachery that had been committed against him and he never would. Anyone that had crossed him, he would *get back*. Anyone that he hadn't dealt with yet was still on his hit list, but Joseph Aku had now been promoted, right to the fucking top.

JOSEPH

Bradley Brown was a fucking prick but he was also fucking right. My heart was pounding inside my chest as if it were a trapped bear trying to get out. I didn't like to think of myself as scared of anyone but Brad was my boy - well had been my boy - so he knew exactly how I'd be feeling right now. Bradley had no clue about the trouble I was in though, and I would bet every last penny that I had, that Bradley wouldn't want to hear of it now, anyway. It was too late. The violation had already been committed and Bradley wanted blood. *My* blood. I can't even go to the shop without one of my children beside me because Brad has always lived by a *no kids allowed* rule. A rule that I was truly grateful for right now.

That's what I'd always liked and admired about Bradley. He was vicious but he was also careful. He didn't do accidental casualties, he was a courteous hitman. A walking oxymoron; Bradley only hurt his rivals and he really did help old ladies cross the road safely or carry their shopping bags to their front door. Obviously not everyone - particularly elderly white ladies - received the offer of assistance with gratitude. Plenty of ladies just clutched their bag tighter, looking highly intimidated, scared. I've felt the same way, many a time around Bradley and that was when we were friends. Brad is tall and wide, has a top row full of gold teeth and wears his hair in dreads. He looks like he's from Chicago, until he opens his mouth and South London jumps out.

I didn't mean to betray Bradley. I mean, I wish I hadn't felt like I'd had to but I honestly didn't really have much choice. I had been desperate. Really desperate and I'd known that if I had told Bradley about my problem, his only suggestion would've been violence. Bradley always chose violence. Always. But he'd also have known that I'd been doing things without him so he would've chosen violence for me too. Now he's going to anyway. He *will* kill me if he catches me alone.

When we were fifteen years old, I didn't mind Bradley's wild, impulsive attitude but we weren't school aged boys any more. We were big men with kids to help raise and I cared about my children even if Mad Brad didn't give a fuck about his. He'd regret it when they grew up to hate him, though. I had two kids and two baby mothers to provide for and although I couldn't stand either of the women, I knew that I was stuck with them for the foreseeable future and that fatherhood didn't come cheap. Sharlene and Sharelle were always after something for my daughters, Deja and Tayjah. I needed shit for myself and my mother too, but I'd been overspending, to stunt and flex and I had been spending profit without leaving enough money to re-up. I had accumulated a lot of debt, by trying to do drug deals without Bradley, in order to have more profit for myself but I had been dealing with the wrong type of connections, and they wanted the money I owed, or they were gonna kill me. I was trapped and desperate. I didn't know what else to do. The holiday was just an excuse to get Bradley away.

It had always been Bradley that dealt with all the business

transactions in the past and I'd had to find people who didn't know or work with Bradley. Without Bradley's protection, I was vulnerable. *Very* vulnerable. Bradley was feared and didn't take any shit from anyone. He'd already been to jail a few times, always returning home with more muscles in his arms and less love in his heart. But as well as a right hook that had left a few people unconscious for a while, Bradley also used weapons like they were pleasantries that he was handing out, stabbing and shooting anyone that upset him. And for trivial things, too. Not that violence was ever the answer, but we all say that until one of ours is hurt.

Bradley's temper could go from zero to one hundred in a millisecond, though. People were scared to upset Mad Brad because his reputation had him down as a deranged madman. He had stabbed his own father for hitting his mother - deliberately in the spine - leaving him permanently paralysed and in a wheelchair. Everyone knew that Bradley had done that, even the police but his father had given the police a different story - one about masked intruders - to spare his son from jail. And probably because the man had been afraid, that if he'd sent his son to prison, Bradley would've just finished him off, once he'd been released.

Bradley had ended up going to jail for something else a month later anyway but it was for something minor. It was always something minor whenever Bradley went to jail, never for the more serious charges like attempted murder and *murder*. He'd always beaten those cases when they'd made it as far as court but most of the serious crimes that Bradley had been arrested for, never even made it that far. They usually ended, NFA - no further action - from the police. But there had always been plenty more action from Bradley, taking care of business on the streets of London.

Some people had started whispering that Bradley must've been snitching to the police or something - to be getting away with so much - but they'd never say that to his face. Bradley had always spoken against snitching and had told me that he'd been buying his way out of jail, like it was just a game of Monopoly, but who knew? Maybe he had been protesting so much against snitching because he was guilty of it. It happened. A lot.

But I knew that I had done the unthinkable - robbing your partner, was right up there with snitching, by street code standards - but I'd convinced myself that Bradley would probably have done the same thing, if he'd been in my position. Loyalty goes out of the window when you're in survival mode but none of this stopped me from being shook to my core. Bradley wouldn't stop calling me and I'd been holed up inside one of my baby mother's house, constantly looking out of the window from behind the net curtain. I knew both of those bitches were in constant contact with the man who wanted me dead. Even while I was right there, with them. They may not have cared about me much, but I was their children's father. Did that not count for anything? I hated those slags. And I'm shook. I'm absolutely terrified of dying and leaving my kids behind. I know that Bradley won't physically hurt them, but they'll surely miss me, if I was gone. And what about my mother? Oh shit, how would my mum cope, if I was just to disappeared?

I knew that I was on borrowed time, unless I could get out of Dodge before Mad Brad finally caught up with me. There was only one thing that I could do. It was the one thing that the streets said, that you weren't supposed to do. Ever.

In the moment of crisis, the wise build bridges, and the

foolish build dams.

I was going to build a bridge but once I'd crossed that particular bridge, there really was, no going back. I would have to build it, set it on fire and then run.

D.S JOHNSON

These young black men - even the school boys - were throwing their lives away, but they were also keeping me employed and busy. Wandsworth police station like many across London, sees a steady stream of youths - not all black but the majority - being charged with possession of firearms and knives. Thankfully most are only nicked for carrying rather than using weapons, but still too many people were being shot and stabbed on my patch. Fortunately, the police do get help from the general public sometimes - otherwise even more crimes would never be solved - but the general consensus amongst the black community was that the police were institutionally racist. That 1999 MacPherson report, really did screw up policing, or at least that is what it was designed to do. But even before that, there was often a wall of silence, whenever it was a black on black crime. That's how it went for one of my unsolved cases - well not just one. But this case was particularly tough to work because even though everyone knew who had done it, nobody was talking. And I mean *nobody*.

A shooting. The murder of a wannabe rapper from North London. Someone who had openly dissed the guy that always seemed to slip through the net. It was me that had used to let that happen, because the person who was affronted by the diss, is a guy that used to grease my palm with lots of his dirty cash, but he has been too fucking trigger happy, for the pleasure. It doesn't fucking look good. The fool! So hopefully this caller and the evidence they have promised to hand over, could be the answer to my prayers. Of course, it was no huge loss when someone like that Channel U star was the victim. He'd been shot whilst riding his motorbike through the Burtop Road Estate in Earlsfield, one night five years ago. It was a case that I thought that I'd never get to court. I had all but given up on it, so this could be a real treat.

The caller allegedly has items of clothing worn by the shooter when he'd committed the murder. The icing on the cake, is that the clothes supposedly have the victim's blood on them. The man on the phone was most definitely nervous and he would be, because the person he's about to rat on, is responsible for a large amount of the criminality, violence and bloodshed on my turf. Someone who I know doesn't take kindly to snitches. He's never done it himself. Instead, he'd always stump up the readies to prevent me going to the Crown Prosecution Service. With the big cases that is. I have to send the piece of shit to prison occasionally, or at least hope that's what the courts decided to do with him, once I'd sent him on to that part of the criminal justice process. He couldn't always afford that privilege, though. He used to be a scrawny little monkey, broke and delinquent, when we were first acquainted. He'd been about thirteen years old, the first time he'd been nicked. I'd known straight away, that he was going to be a regular at my Hotel for Justice. Only his size and finances have changed since then. He'll *always* be a delinquent, monkey.

Often these imbeciles get themselves, before we get them;

they're really doing us a favour, by taking each other out. It's when innocent people, children and coppers get hit - caught in the crossfire - that's when it becomes a problem. That's when I get really angry but it's never been the case with these guys. They have a *no kids allowed* rule but I don't give a fuck who they hit, I will be going for a conviction either way. Unless of course, they can afford to buy their way out of it. But there are limits and you've got to use your fucking discretion. Not go around, *popping* people, willy-nilly like they're back in fucking Africa. But when they kill one of their own and we capture and convict the killer, it's a two for one offer; kill two birds with one stone. One dead and the other behind bars for a nice stretch. It doesn't make any real difference on our streets though, because there are still much more of them on the streets than behind prison walls, but it does makes my job more enjoyable. And it's what I am paid to do.

I can see my informant and his children, feeding the ducks at the pond in the park, in total disregard to the sign that clearly forbids people to do so. This is how it starts off. Disobeying simple rules and teaching your children to do the same. Those two girls will probably end up in gangs themselves, just like their mother and father before them. Trust me when I confirm for you that the apple doesn't fall far from the tree, because I've seen it in my nearly twenty years on the Force; it's only gotten worse and it was getting worse still. When I retire, my wife, children and I will be moving far away from shitty London. Somewhere in the countryside, somewhere that isn't so liberal and multicultural. Look how that's going with this place - to pot - that's how. Mark my words, by the year twenty thirty, London will be in the top five most dangerous cities in the world. My family and I will not be sticking around to see it.

There are some decent black folk but the bad apples make the rest of the fruit look spoiled, too. That's just how life goes, I'm afraid. I don't make the rules but if I did, it would only take one serious act of violence from them to have them locked away for the rest of their lives. Because their beef never ends. It's non stop carnage even as they age and have families of their own. They still go tit for tat, settling old scores, because they have more pride than sense. Fucking idiots!

Ignorance can be cured, but stupidity is forever.

I walk past a white family with children feeding the ducks and smile at the beautiful sight. Of course it's different, when *we* do it. It just is!

BRADLEY

Bradley still hadn't managed to catch Joseph on his own. He'd been posted outside Sharlene's house for a whole twenty four hours, having demanded that she leave with her daughter. She had done as she was told and gone over to her cousin's house. Bradley had then taken a few shots at her living room window, when he'd thought that he'd seen a shadow and then he'd sped off in his car before a concerned citizen had the chance to send the police on his tail. Sharlene had since confirmed upon returning home, that the only thing Bradley had damaged, apart from the obvious window pane, was her interior walls and her sofa. Both had been struck by bullets but Joseph had remained unharmed.

Bradley was fuming. Joseph was really mugging him off. He hadn't even tried to apologise or explain himself since the robbery had gone down. He was still airing Bradley's calls and texts and the longer it went on, the angrier Bradley was getting. It was a surprise that steam wasn't coming out of his ears and now Bradley found himself wondering, whether Joseph had been up to no good from way before this. There was no way this was a one off; Bradley was now questioning everything. He'd never queried Joseph about it, if the product - the drugs - or the cash was light by anything under a hundred pounds because

Bradley knew that shit happened. Sometimes you'd give a bit extra to a regular or even take a few lines for yourself, but if Joseph had stolen eighty pounds from their stash every day for a month, Bradley estimated that Joseph could've easily stolen over two thousand pounds each month, from their profit. That was twenty four thousand pounds that Joseph could've accumulated, in a year. That was a lot of money, and Bradley was mad at himself for not being more cautious, more discerning. He should've learned not to trust *anyone*, by now.

Bradley had wanted to believe that Joseph was innocent; he hadn't wanted to accept that he'd been fooled by his friend, but in his heart, Bradley knew that was the reality, the truth. He'd never had any reason to doubt that Joseph was anything but good people, before the stash house robbery, but now the whole fourteen years of their friendship was questionable. Bradley couldn't put anything past that guy, now; Joseph had put him in a lot of debt, and although Bradley had the means to replace the product - and make his money back if he laced it with some boric acid - it was still a loss, and a fucking violation and Bradley was known for having high purity cocaine. He didn't usually cut his cocaine. He kept his customers happy, so that they kept coming back for more. Bradley didn't sell to them though, he had runners for that; the *youngers* that were now doing what he was doing, ten years ago, with Joseph. Now Bradley was on standby to kill his his one-time, closest friend. Bradley was still in shock but he *was* going to kill Joseph as soon as he caught him slipping, then he'd help auntie Aku, pay for her son's funeral. Which Bradley would attend, wearing the snake's face on a tee shirt. Bradley even fantasised about cutting out the middle man and cremating the pussy himself. Burning the little pussy, alive. Bradley could wait forever and a day for Joseph but he was hungry for the man's blood right now. He'd had others watching out for Joseph too but he really wanted this body for himself.

Something was making Bradley feel anxious though. He texted his mother to make sure she was okay, at work. Once she'd texted back that she was fine, Bradley sat down on his bed and practised the breathing exercises that he'd been taught by one of the nicer teachers that he'd met, during his short era of education. Joseph wasn't going out without one or both of his kids in tow and everybody knew that Bradley would never strike wherever children were at. He'd always said that anyone's fair game, *except* kids and Bradley or anyone doing a job for him, would always stand down if children were present. Joseph was aware of that fact more than anyone and had taken his children out more times in the past week, than he ever had before.

Bradley wanted the money that Joseph owed him and then he was going to take that pussy's life. Joseph had already owed Bradley about ten thousand pounds and now he owed him much more than he could afford to repay. If he could, then surely Joseph would not have stolen from him in the first place. Joseph denying his involvement and thinking that Bradley wouldn't suspect him because they were together at the time, just made Bradley more vexed. Did Joseph really think that he was that much of a dickhead? He hadn't given Bradley any money towards anything for months. Bradley had even stored some cocaine and cash in his safe inside his wardrobe at his mother's house and he didn't usually leave anything incriminating at home. Something had made Bradley wary of leaving all of his shit in the stash house though, and he would've lost a lot more if he hadn't trusted his instincts. Something had told him to be wary of Joseph and he'd been right to.

What was Joseph really on, though? It infuriated Bradley that the pagan was still breathing. How could Joseph do what he'd done to Bradley and still sleep at night? And people said that Bradley didn't have a heart! He had levels that he just wouldn't sink to and near the top of that list was snitching, taking out kids - not even with a stray bullet - and robbing his fucking friends. Bradley had heard of and seen too many children end up with life changing injuries, some had even lost their life because pagans didn't give a fuck about who they hit, and had either let off gun shots or swung swords in the vicinity of children. Bradley would always stand down if his target was with or near kids. He might not be much of a father to his own but he lived by that rule and he wished that everybody else did too.

People had often asked Bradley, why he was so passionate about not hurting children, and he'd thought that it was fucking obvious but he would later connect it to a childhood trauma. Bradley could never endorse Joseph being taken out whilst out with one or both of his children; he was already going to take their father away from them, they were already going to suffer because of their father's actions. They didn't need to witness his execution too or be hurt in the process. Mad Brad weren't all bad, people just didn't get him but he preferred it that way. Joseph had proven to him, that even your tightest bro would fuck you over, whenever they felt like it. Bradley had learned that lesson from a really young age, but it hadn't stopped it from happening to him again. Many times, in fact. That was the reason why he hadn't entertained any friend apart from Joseph, in the first place. Unless they had been riding out with the SUK gang, it had always just been Bradley and Joseph or Bradley on his own. He had even cut off his relatives, and didn't talk to anyone on his father or mother's side, now that both his maternal grandparents were dead. His mother's parent's had been a comfort to him in his childhood; even when his behaviour was destructive and extreme, apart from a lecture when he visited them, they had always shown Bradley love and patience. He used to stay with them at weekends and during the school holidays before he started yearning for the streets. He still missed them, even though, his gran had been dead for six years, outliving her husband, by two years. Now Bradley wished that he hadn't let his guard down with Joseph because it was only *himself,* whom he could trust and rely on. His mother too, to a certain extent.

Bradley pondered for the millionth time, about whom it was that Joseph had used to rob him. If he didn't find out before he caught up with that snake, Joseph was going to get a bullet for them two pussies as well. Then once he'd taken Joseph out, Bradley would have to go away for a while. Lay low and wait to hear if the police were on to him. His bag was packed and ready to go; he would miss his mother but she wasn't built for a life on the run. He wouldn't be away for too long. He did this whenever he had to, so his mother was used to it by now. But that wouldn't stop her from worrying, so Bradley always bought a cheap phone and a pay as you go SIM, whenever he took off. He'd usually only given the number to his mother and Joseph, but now Bradley's whole life had changed. Two had become one and it wasn't anything to do with the Spice Girls. *But I will be Scary Spice when I catch you, Aku,* Bradley laughed to himself.

Joseph had stolen from him, instead of asking him for a favour, like the big fucking man he had always claimed to be. Bradley felt confused by Joseph's actions, as well as hurt and betrayed but to the outside world, he only ever showed his anger. Unfortunately for Bradley, he would soon realise, that Joseph was not done with the violations just yet. Just as he was getting ready to go and hunt the snake again, the police were forcing entry to Bradley's home, to arrest him. For murder. And this time they had evidence. That pussy Joseph had kept hold of Bradley's clothing which he'd ask him to dispose of, expecting Joseph to burn them or discard them or something. Anything but keep them and give them to the police. But if Joseph had kept Bradley's clothing for all this time, five years, he'd obviously been entertaining plans to set Bradley up, for a while.

Bradley shook his head and then put his hands on top of it as he heard the front door crash open. Then came the shouts of *armed police,* followed immediately by lots of footsteps storming up the stairs, towards his bedroom. Bradley's dad, Delroy, in his wheelchair in the hallway on the ground floor, shouts, *a wha di bloodclaart?* to no one in particular. Meanwhile upstairs, Bradley is roughed up and cuffed up, by a group of armed police officers in helmets and tactical gear. All the while, Bradley is astonished that Joseph could've done this to him. Snitching was never the way but Bradley shouldn't have been surprised, because Joseph Aku was nothing but a pussy. A fucking thieving, snitching, pussy at that. Snitching was *never* cool. How fucking dare Joseph! Bradley really couldn't believe it but he looked up to the ceiling and thanked God, because he had removed everything from his home earlier that day, otherwise he would've lost even more money.

As the police led him out and away from his home in Battersea, Bradley felt sorry for his mother. He'd promised her that he'd get his life in order, but she knew what he was doing; it came with the territory, really. It was a daily hazard of having an illegal occupation. But Bradley would be back. It might not be tomorrow, it might not be for a while, but Bradley knew one thing for certain. One way or another, Joseph Aku was dead!

A patient man rides a donkey.

Bradley would have plenty of time on his hands now, but Joseph did not - his days were numbered. Bradley would walk out of prison a free man one day, but Joseph would be long dead. Bradley would bet his whole life on that.

II

2011

YOU SHAKE A MAN'S HAND, NOT HIS HEART

The person that presents themselves to you, may not be genuine

JOSEPH

It's been nearly two years since Bradley got *bagged*. He's sent me plenty of warnings via social media and through people who were once my friends and associates. I was alienated for being a snitch and had to leave London swiftly because Bradley had put a price on my head. Now I cant even see my kids. It's not safe. It may never be safe for me. This is why we don't snitch; because it ruins your fucking life and witness protection isn't offered like it is on television, in real life. Not to people like me, anyway. A train ticket to a backwater Bed and Breakfast, is about the best we'll get. It makes me wonder everyday, if it was worth it. Getting rid of Bradley was meant to be beneficial for me but even though it essentially saved my life, I'm no longer free to live where and how I want to. I don't really have much of a life, at all now.

The trial was an absolute nightmare. I had hoped that Bradley would just plead guilty, knowing that he was cornered with the evidence that would be presented to a jury by the prosecution, but knowing Bradley, he'd probably only opted for a trial, just to eyeball me. Just to make me even more scared than I had been, ever since I'd witnessed his reaction to the robbery, in Zante. Bradley had gotten us thrown out of the club because he had thrown a bottle of Cristal in the direction of no one in particular. We'd already paid for and drunk the majority of it but it was obvious to anyone at the time, that Bradley was about to blow a gasket. I'd needed Bradley locked up, to save myself. If Bradley was a free man, I'd have been dead already. I needed him to stay in prison this time. It was his own fault. He shouldn't have been gunning for me like that.

I opted to give my evidence via video camera, so Bradley didn't get to eyeball me anyway. Yes, I am a coward and a thief. Bradley had goons in the gallery, that were simply there to intimidate and scare me, too. I hadn't actually been there at the time of the murder that Bradley was on trial for. Bradley did that job and many others, solo, but he'd come to see me after the act. My first child had been born just a few weeks before and I had decided that the street lifestyle, was no longer for me. I was going to keep selling drugs to feed my family, but I was done with all the other shit. I was twenty years old, a father to a beautiful baby girl and I wasn't going to do dumb shit and leave my daughter without her father; soon that became daughters, four years later, with the birth of my second child. I also didn't want to leave my mother without her son. I was all she had. But I had to leave my mother and both of my daughter's in the end because it just wasn't safe for me.

My mum was stuck in her ways and would never have agreed to, or coped with, a life on the run. I couldn't tell her the real reason I had to go. My parents knew that I got into fights and that I sometimes carried a weapon for my own protection, because those are the offences that I'd been arrested for. My parents would've thrown me out of the house, if they had known that I was making my money, from selling hard drugs. I had bought a MacBook and told them that I was a Junior investor. It's the only way they'd take the money that I was making, partly for my parent's benefit anyway. My mum doesn't know that I gave evidence to the police and in court, against Bradley. She thinks that Bradley is living in Jamaica. He has called her many times from jail, to say *how bodi.* I knew that Bradley wouldn't physically hurt my mother, but he did hurt her, by forcing us to separate from each other. By making me run because he was going to kill me. Bradley was a father too but he had never been interested in being any sort of decent father, so he wouldn't have understood what it was like for me to abandon my fatherly duties. His attitude had always been, I told her I didn't want it. Bradley just didn't care about anybody. He even treated his own mother like shit but hated it when his dad did the same.

We had been cool back in the day, but Bradley had always been a fool; recklessly stabbing people for no real reason. Bradley's brain was like a Nigerian party without jollof - something was definitely missing. Well, he would have the next thirty years to get his head right and by then he would be too old and too afraid to go back to jail, to do anything to me. Thirty years was a long time. Anything could happen, but life will have definitely moved on. Bradley should've moved on too by then but right now I'm not safe and the police are not doing anything to change that. They'd just discarded me like a used serviette, once I'd given evidence; sharing the details of Bradley's confession on the night that he'd killed the North London rapper.

Protected behind a screen, I'd recalled how Bradley had relived the shooting - demonstrating to me, exactly what he'd done. Where and how he'd left the body; and how Bradley had taken the victim's motorbike and left it outside the victim's mother's house, a few days after the shooting. As a result of doing all of that, I'd had to leave my mother, my daughters, and my whole world, behind. I speak to my mother, occasionally and we both say *I dey fine,* but I can't trust my baby mother's, so I do not have any contact with them or my girls. The women would probably betray me, because Bradley's money and therefore power, was stronger and longer, than their loyalty to me. Bradley had probably fucked both of those hoes anyway. If only he knew what they were *really* like. I missed my little girls but if I tried to see them, it would probably be the very last thing that I did, so in the end, I'd decided to just cut my losses and leave.

I've asked my mum to keep an eye on my girls for me, but she's not been too well. She's said it's nothing serious but she doesn't sound herself and I'm really worried about her. If anything happens to her before it's safe for me to go home, I swear I'll find a way to hurt Bradley, or someone he loves, but I hope my mum will be okay. I intend to pray everyday and ask God to keep her safe and well and then I'll make a new life for myself and hope that Bradley won't find me. In a few years time, when Bradley would've calmed down and realised that I was just protecting myself and that he'd left me with no choice, I would return home, or make things easier for my mother to join me, wherever I am. I haven't told her the real reason I've had to run; she doesn't even know that Bradley wants me dead. He's even had the audacity to send her money and he's in prison. I cant afford to do that because I need every penny that I have.

Thankfully, Bradley Brown was a loud mouth fool, so it wasn't too hard to know when and where, I was being hunted. I hoped that it stayed that way; I was constantly checking social media, knowing that Bradley always seemed to have access to a phone, when in prison. I had made several fake accounts on various apps, to spy on the people that were trying to find me.

A roaring Lion, kills no game.

Bradley's arrogance was helping me stay hidden. I was keeping it moving. I would eventually settle wherever I felt that I could. I knew where not to go, though, because of the things I saw online. Soon I'd be gone for good. Joseph will no longer exist. The person Bradley is chasing, is already dead to me. It was time to reinvent myself. Goodbye, Joseph. Hello, Shane.

BRADLEY

Bradley had now been banged up for more than two years, and it had been an eye opening experience for him. He'd been to jail a few times before but he had never received a sentence longer than four years prior to this one, and in most cases in the UK, you'd only serve half of your given sentence, so Bradley had never really been away for more than a couple of years. Usually with a few additional days on his sentences for infractions committed inside whatever prison he was incarcerated.

Mad Brad had already been sent to the block - or the segregation unit as its properly known - many times since he'd been nicked for shooting some dickhead from North London. The prick had made a diss track with the bar: *I don't care if he's mad, I don't give a fuck if he cheffed his dad.* Now imprisoned, Bradley was having to deal with rivals from North, West, East and South London and that meant that Mad Brad, just couldn't stop fighting. No way was he getting filmed like all them dickheads getting treated like a bitch, and posted on socials for all to see. No fucking way. But things would soon change.

Once Bradley had been sentenced, he'd been moved to HMP Parkhurst on the Isle of Wight and although it was a mission for his family and close associates to visit, it was a much better place to be. Bradley had been in some of the worst rat infested, gloomy, hell-holes back on the mainland. He didn't have many people that would actually visit him anyway. But Bradley had other more useful business to deal with, than fighting the fools he was banged up with. Yes, he would fuck up any and everybody, if he needed to - Bradley didn't care if it was one man or ten and everybody knew that - but there was plenty of money to be made in prison.

The time that one spent banged up, could be beneficial, if you knew what you were doing and Bradley considered himself to be a pro at this, now. He had a lot of influence both inside and outside of the jail and his operation was set up and ready to go. Bradley could now supply all of the wings with whatever they needed and wanted; drugs to sell or drugs to take, except spice. He wanted no association with that zombie drug. Bradley knew that a lot of dealers, were also consumers of their own product and he was no exception, but he had self control and pride. He had limits and wouldn't touch certain substances even if he was paid. Spice was producing a subgroup of crazies and Bradley wanted no part of that. He didn't sell the stuff because he didn't even like being around people who indulged in it but it was commonplace in most prisons.

Bradley had seen too many people dabble, then get dabbed - meaning that they'd once had control of their drug of choice but eventually and sometimes very quickly, the drug took control, over them. Now Bradley was about to start doing what he loved to do whenever he was locked up; distribute drugs at a highly inflated price. Sometimes more than ten times the street value. Commodities in prison didn't come cheap and he had always made the most of that fact whenever he was doing time. He had just under twenty eight years left to stack his paper up and leave prison a lot more well off than when he went in.

Bradley had used the time in jail so far to bond with all of his children and all of their mothers too. As soon as he'd gotten a mobile phone, he'd been requesting pornographic FaceTimes, and every single one of the bitches, had obliged. Bradley felt like, the man. Yes, he knew that the women would all be getting the real deal from dudes, who still had their freedom, but as long as Bradley got his entertainment and they did as he asked, he didn't give a fuck about all of that. If it was the other way around, Bradley knew that he wouldn't be waiting for any bitch. Life was too short for all that bullshit. Bradley thought that girls were just dumb bitches anyway, but that had always worked in his favour, and it was no different, now.

Even though contraband was often taken into the prisons by the prison officers - the screws - and by drones or by people simply throwing packages over the high, barbed wire topped walls, it was still via visitation that plenty of drugs and other prohibited items got through the prison gates. It was lucrative if you knew what you were doing. Bradley's eldest child was already eleven years old, having fathered him, when he was just sixteen. The child's mother had only been fourteen at the time and Bradley hadn't thought that, that was a big deal but he had denied having sex with the girl, anyway. He had instead told everyone except his mother, that she had only given him, head but Candace had always known the truth; Kano had been born looking very much like his, father. Years later Bradley had retracted and admitted that the girl had in fact been telling the truth but he had never issued her an apology. Until he'd gone to jail this time, that is. Then, he had been all apologetic and begging for a chance to build a relationship with his son. Thankfully, Hoey Khloe had been all for it. She had jumped at the opportunity to give Bradley some live, pornographic, camera action too, even though she had stated from the very start of her communication with him in jail, that she *did* have a boyfriend.

That was just *one* of the reason that Bradley didn't have serious relationships, with girls; they were all snakey hoes, as far as he was concerned. He didn't trust any woman apart from his mother, and even she, had let him down a couple of times. She was always there for him when he needed her, though. Bradley didn't usually forgive people and he never, ever forgot about a betrayal but Bradley and his mother had been getting on so much better, right before he'd come to jail. Bradley could've bought his own house, but he had chosen to pay off his mother's mortgage and stay at home, in hers. He had given - or at least offered - his mother, plenty of money, for her to carry on treating him like she always had. Shopping, cooking and cleaning for him. It wasn't his fault, that his mother didn't like to take his money. Bradley did his own laundry and his mother could not go into his bedroom, which he had always kept locked and she had never complained. When things were good between them, she was the best mum Bradley could have asked for and he was glad that his father couldn't raise a single thing to hit her any more but occasionally, he thought he could understand why his dad had used to put his hands on her. The woman really could be, very fucking, annoying.

Bradley had wanted his father out of their house but his mother had begged him, to let the useless piece of shit stay. She loved that man no matter what, but Bradley had to remind himself that his mum had also forgiven him plenty of times and he had done some shit to her that he had lived to regret, too. Bradley had been a tough kid in his younger years; kicked out of primary school for bad behaviour - his mum had tried to home school him but he had just walked out of the house, ignoring her protests, most days. He had only been ten years old. He'd later been allowed to enrol in a few secondary schools, after his mother had fought his case, but Bradley had ended up being permanently excluded from all of them. He'd actually been quite a smart boy, but he'd never had any social skills and he didn't want to be social, either. Bradley hated everyone. His dad, especially. He reckoned that the violence he'd witnessed his father inflict on his mother, had left him mentally fucked up. Bradley blamed his dad for *everything*. He just could not stand, that little piece of shit. Now Bradley would be footing the bill for the carers that his dad needed, until that sad, pathetic invalid, was dead, and finally out of their lives for good.

His mother had been adamant that she'd give up work and care for the cretin, full-time, herself but Bradley would never have allowed that, to happen. His mother had chosen to carry on working her job as a Personal Assistant to a banking executive in the city, rather than depend on Bradley's illegal gains, because she liked being independent. He couldn't allow his mother to sacrifice her freedom and salary, for that worthless man. A man who'd never worked a day in his life. A man who had always begged and stolen from her, whilst his mother had always worked so hard, to provide for the three of them. Bradley often wondered how his mother had settled with such a man, but she'd always say to him, *you wouldn't be you, without your father, Bradley.* Bradley wished now, that he had just ended Delroy's life, when he'd had the chance, since he was going to end up serving a life sentence anyway.

Bradley didn't know where Joseph Aku was right now but Bradley had plenty of time on his hands to find out. And he *would* find him. Bradley had met Joseph at his first secondary school, before he had been kicked out, and Joseph had been the only boy from that school, or any of the others, that Bradley had stayed in touch with. They didn't live too far from each other in Battersea, so they had chilled together in the evenings, when Joseph was back from school and at the weekends when Joseph had been allowed out. Then they had started running with the SUK guys, robbing people and patrolling the *ends*. Sometimes Bradley had carried a knife, but once he was fifteen and one of the older's of the crew had gifted him a gun, Bradley had been trigger happy, ever since. He'd used the same handgun so many times - against the advice of people who thought that they knew best - that Bradley had to be grateful now, that he was only serving *one*, life sentence. One of his victim's bodies, had never been found, but you'd never know because you don't see many stories on primetime television, about missing black people. And there were plenty of them. Bradley wasn't complaining, though. That suited him just fine; if no one was looking, then nothing could be found, and the police wouldn't be able to convict him for anything else.

Bradley knew that racism both helped him, and hindered him as a criminal. He could get away with doing things to certain people; the people who like him, hated the police, because of how differently white criminals were treated compared to their black counterparts, so they would never report crimes committed against them. He could also harm other criminals, people the police saw as degenerate, and didn't care too much about. At the same time, he'd regularly been getting arrested, ever since he'd turned thirteen, whilst the rich white guys who he bought the drugs from, lived in big detached houses in the countryside, drove luxury cars and never or rarely ever, got pulled over, much less, harassed and arrested on a regular basis, by the police. But that was just life, though. Bradley accepted things for what they were, and he just tried to make the best of his personal circumstances. He couldn't and wouldn't attempt to change the world.

He'd once been chased and beaten by a group of white men, wearing Chelsea insignia, after a big home game at Stamford Bridge. Living on the poor side of the bridges that separated the rich and poor in that part of London, had been weird for Bradley growing up. He couldn't understand how he could simply walk over three bridges - Battersea, Albert and Chelsea - and be in a completely different environment. Even though the football hooligans had really left Bradley, battered with a skull fracture, broken wrist and two cracked ribs, Bradley had refused to give a statement to the police. He just didn't do that. Ever. It was after that experience though, that Bradley and Joseph had joined a gang.

Now, Bradley couldn't get his head around the fact that his oldest, his only friend, had robbed him. Snitched on him, handed over evidence to the police and got him nabbed for *this* murder. So now on top of a lot of money, Joseph Aku had stolen thirty years of Bradley's life. And Joseph was going to pay the price, by losing *his* life. As soon as he'd been sniffed out. Bradley's craving for vengeance was just as intense now as it had been, when he'd watched the lick happening, back in Zante, more than two years ago. Probably much stronger, if Bradley was honest. Time was not a healer for Bradley and he was not just going to let what Joseph had done to him, slide. He had six different women that he'd fathered kids to and about four other stupid hoes that he could employ on rotation, to satisfy his sexual desires and Bradley felt as though his life wasn't all that bad for a guy that was doing a thirty year bid behind bars.

Bradley would bet, that wherever that pussy Joseph Aku was, he didn't have as much money and hoes as he did, and it was him who was locked up. Bonus points were awarded to Bradley by himself because he had Joseph's two daughter's, calling him Dad and their mother's called him daddy, whilst using sex toys on camera for him. Yes, Bradley definitely felt as though things weren't really that bad, at all. The only thing that could've made it better, was if Joseph Aku, could fucking watch. He'd sent a video to the pussy's old Facebook account anyway, just in case he was still checking it, from wherever he was hiding. He texted his mother on his mother on the Blackberry that he'd paid a lot of money for, and asked her to transfer one thousand pounds to auntie Aku.

* * *

Bradley grabbed Khloe for a hug, quickly and forcefully, putting his hands down her jeans to retrieve his package. He didn't have time to try and play with the other package that she had hidden down there but he'd enjoy the smell of it on his treasure, later. Khloe introduces Bradley to his eldest child, his son Kano, who had looked just as terrified as his mother, as the boy had watched the stranger, that was his father, put his hand near his mother's private parts. Bradley had felt a bit guilty about putting his son and his mother through that but it was necessary and he was going to get Kano an Xbox 360 and a few pairs of Air Jordan's. Khloe already knew that Bradley would make it worth her while; he'd already sent her a lot of money since he'd been locked up.

Bradley still had money on the outside. His mum was holding onto that for him. He knew that he could trust her, with that. She could help herself but she rarely did and she always used her discretion. Candace Brown was many things but she was never greedy; using her own income primarily and Bradley's contributions for her occasional treats. Luxuries that she wouldn't otherwise be able to afford, after her regular monthly bills were taken care of. Bradley had often forced money on his mother; Candace had always told him that his obligations were to his children not his parents but Bradley had never, and would never give Delroy, a single penny of his money. Paying for the cripple's care, was done with much resentment, and for his mother's sake, only. Candace did take money from Bradley for his children, though. Some of which she saved in accounts for them, whilst the rest, she handed directly to their mothers. Bradley really respected his mother for that. But that was all that Bradley's mother did for him; managed his funds - whether he was at home, or away in jail - his mother held his money in various bank accounts. He wasn't sure how or what his mum did to prevent the police confiscating his livelihood but she knew a lot of different types of people and her best friend was an accountant. Bradley would never have let his mother have contact with the drugs. Yes, he would've been worried about her getting caught but he was also concerned about his crackhead father, bullying her into handing it over. His mother wasn't stupid, she knew what he did but she didn't approve. She just also knew, that Bradley had started making his own disastrous decisions, at a very young age, before he'd even hit puberty; it was pointless repeating the same lectures to him as man, that he had always ignored as a boy.

Khloe had looked really pretty on the visit; she was all grown up now. Bradley had thought hundreds of times over the years, that the fact that Khloe had always been very forward for her age, should've went in his favour when he'd gotten her pregnant at fourteen years old. He was not a kiddy-feeler and Khloe had said that she was sixteen at the time. Did he know she was lying? Probably. He had confided in his mother and she had contacted Khloe, and apologised on his behalf. Candace had been visiting Kano since he was a baby and had at one stage, she had been financially supporting Khloe, out of her own pocket.

Bradley didn't have money when he was sixteen, but as soon as his mother knew that he could more than afford it, she'd demanded money to set aside in an account for her first grandchild. She'd opened an account for Kano and told Bradley, that she thought, that he didn't want to be like his father. That had really stung, but it had made Bradley hand over the money, regularly and without protest. Candace had cursed plenty of bad words - words that Bradley hadn't even thought his mother knew - when he had told her a few years later, that she was a grandmother, at least four times over. He'd soon regretted telling her though, because she had demanded to know the details of all the girls who may, or may not have been the mother of his children, and proceeded to open savings accounts for *all* of the children.

Candace had told Bradley - even before she had discovered that she was a grandmother - that if a man ever had reason to believe, that he *could* be the father of a woman's child, it meant that they were not being responsible or careful. It was therefore, in Candace's opinion, Bradley's duty, to prove that he wasn't the father, or he would have to pay the consequences. Literally. Bradley hadn't bothered with doing any DNA tests, because he'd had no intention of being a father, back then, even if the tests had confirmed that he was.

Candace enforcing Bradley's financial responsibility to his children, didn't actually make him more responsible, at all. That had been her way of trying to do right by her grandchildren and it had suited Bradley, because it meant that she left him alone and didn't stress him out about, actually visiting his children and spending *time* with them. Parting with his paper, his money, had been too easy for Bradley. By then, he could more than afford to do so, and it was pocket change to him, once he'd turned eighteen and people had started taking him more, seriously. Drugs were high value goods; kids were used to traffic the stuff and carry out slave labour, assisting the operation of county lines, but nobody trusted a school boy to handle large amounts of drugs or money. By the age of twenty, Bradley was well connected in the class A drug distribution, in South London and he could more than afford to bestow several hundred pounds, upon a few young, single mothers each month. What he couldn't afford to do, was spend time with one child, never mind four and he'd had absolutely no desire to. Candace hadn't actually taught Bradley anything by doing what she'd done, but nevertheless, he was now extremely grateful, that his mother had done right by his children, even when he had not.

Kano was at the age where he needed guidance. Bradley didn't want any of his children ending up in the same position that he was in right now. Not everyone spared kids like Bradley and his associates and in a weird way, Bradley saw that him being a shit father, may have saved his children's lives, because none of his enemies knew who the fuck his children were. Except Joseph, but Bradley wasn't worried about Joseph. He knew that that pussy would never touch his kids; he was not brave enough to go there. Bradley's own father was a proper dickhead and a waste of space, as far as he was concerned. A fucking crackhead. An embarrassment; now a cripple too. Bradley didn't think he was anything like Delroy, and he was ashamed of himself for not being a better father to his own children, when he'd still been a free man.

Delroy had been a junkie since Bradley was a baby, he'd started off as a dealer and had gradually ended up, smoking more crack, than he sold; robbing family, beating his woman. Bradley couldn't understand why his mother hadn't left the man, years ago. Delroy probably thought that Candace was a dumb bitch, the same way that Bradley thought of all women, but that was where the similarities between the two men ended, in Bradley's opinion. He also supposed, that if his mother was going to be a dumb bitch, then it was probably better that it was just for one man, and not lots of different men. He just really wished, that his father was somebody else. Somebody less embarrassing. His mother probably thought that all men were the same, and maybe they were, but her husband, Delroy Brown, was the worst of the worst.

Kano seemed like a smart kid. He was in year eight at Graveney school, in Tooting. At his age, Bradley had already been arrested for assault, possession of drugs and possession of a bladed weapon. Kano didn't need to be doing any of that, though. Bradley had better plans for his first born, child. He wanted all of his children, out of London as soon as possible, because the city wasn't a safe place to be and it was only getting worse. Even though he had never taken a hit around kids, there were plenty of others that didn't care about all of that and it was, *get out the way, or get hit by a stray.*

Some people even hurt their rival's children deliberately, but no matter how mad they said Brad was, you'd never catch him doing, *that.* He may not have been much of a dad before getting *lifed off,* but Bradley had seen and corrected the error of his ways. He was bonding with his children, now. He was trying to anyway, but he knew it would take time. That was okay, because Bradley had plenty of time to kill. If anyone ever tried to hurt any of his kids, he'd find a way to get them from inside. He could and would do that with Joseph, one day.

Bradley knew that Joseph would be forever wondering when he was going to strike, knowing that Bradley - or someone working for him - would eventually find him, and end his existence. This cat and mouse game was was one that Bradley had played many times before, with many different people. As a teenager, he used to rush to avenge the wrongs committed against him, acting on impulse and fueled by rage. The result being that everybody would know it was him that had carried out the lick or the attack and he'd get arrested, or be at risk of reprisal. It didn't matter that he could pay his way out of jail, sometimes. Look at where he was now. Serving a thirty year life sentence, which meant that Bradley would forever be on the police's radar. They now had a legitimate reason to stop and search him, not that they'd ever need one.

Bradley, would never really be free, not even after serving his recommended minimum sentence. He definitely wasn't planning on getting any extra days on this one but he would be on licence for the rest of his life. He would be monitored, until the day that his life ended. So far Bradley had been fortunate enough to receive minor sanctions, for the infractions that he had been caught committing, whilst serving his life term - but like every other privilege within the system, it had cost him. And these privileges were not cheap. Bent screws were like the mafia, controlling who has access to prohibited items in jail, as well as who got away with breaking the rules, and who was written up and reported for their defiance. As long as he didn't get caught by a screw, who was a fucking jobsworth,

Bradley would be making a lot of money very soon. In fact, he already had orders. The payments would be sent to an account in his mother's name. She would then text back the reference to confirm it had been received. The phone he'd left hidden in his cell, would be popping, popping soon and Bradley couldn't wait.

Bradley definitely didn't want this life for any of his children though; three boys and five girls; two of his daughters, he had gained, rather than produced. They were the children that he claimed, anyway. He had standards. He would smash just about anything, but after he came, he was gone. Cum and gone was the best way to be with certain types of females. They were clapped and nobody wanted a child with them. Khloe wasn't clapped though, far from it. All of Bradley's chosen baby mother's were an eight to ten without wearing make up in his opinion and thankfully all of his children had good hair. Not a pepper grain in sight. Kano had even started growing dreads, to look just like his dad and Bradley was glad that the boy had forgiven him for not being there for the first eleven years of his life. And for the way that he had treated his mother; they'd both been young but Bradley had been cruel and immature in his dealings with Khloe back then.

Bradley himself, hated how Delroy had treated his own mother, even causing her to miscarry what would've been his younger sister, when Bradley was just four years old. He'd seen his own father push his mum down the stairs, then he'd lied to the paramedics and said that his mother had tripped and fell. She had suffered broken bones and a serious concussion but the worst news was that she'd lost her baby. Candace had had to give birth to a child that would never get the chance to take its first breath, outside of her womb. Bradley had hated that man a bit more everyday after that and his mother had changed too. She'd given up on her chance of a second child, when Delroy had gone back to using drugs - stealing from her and impregnating skanky, scrawny crackhead, hoes. Those were not Bradley's siblings as far as he was concerned. He was an only child in his eyes and that's how it suited him.

Delroy was vermin as far as Bradley was concerned and the man was only alive, because Candace *was* a dumb bitch. But she would never steal from Bradley; she was the only person he trusted to handle his money on the outside. Bradley had noticed that his mother had been much happier, ever since he had stabbed Delroy, and taught him a lesson about beating his wife. Delroy had robbed Candace of the chance to have a daughter and Bradley had been robbed of the chance to be a big brother. He had never and would never, forgive the man for that. It was whilst in Feltham Young Offenders Institution in his late teens, that a therapist had suggested, that the reason Bradley hated when gang members hurt innocent children so much, could be linked to the trauma he experienced, when he lost his baby sister. Bradley didn't usually believe in all that psychological bullshit, but he'd actually thought, that what they'd said, had made sense.

His mother may have initially been upset and angry about what Bradley had done to him but once she had realised that Delroy would not die but would instead have a life changing injury, Bradley could see that his mum was grateful that her dirty John Crow husband, couldn't beat her anymore. He had done it when Bradley was a kid and it had fucked Bradley up in the head and even at twelve years old, when Delroy had returned from a three year stretch for possession with intent to supply class A drugs, and had started beating his mother all over again, Bradley had vowed to teach his father a lesson one day, and he had. If Bradley said he was going to get you back, then that's exactly what he was going to do. Revenge had no expiry date as far as Bradley was concerned and Joseph had better bare that in mind.

Day is longer than rope.

Patience was something you had to develop, when you were a recidivist like Bradley Brown, and he had plenty of time to kill but Joseph was on borrowed time, to live. The day would soon come when Joseph's life, would be extinguished, but Bradley's lust for vengeance, never would.

Bradley hoped that Joseph was making the most of his life now, wherever he was, because it was definitely temporary. Short term, at that. Joseph wouldn't live to grow old; Bradley would make sure that, Joseph was reunited with his mum and dad, much sooner than Joseph or his parents would have hoped or expected. If Joseph had thought, that time would've simmered Bradley's hate towards him, or that Bradley would've forgiven him in time, for everything that he had done, then he was even more of a fool than Bradley had come to believe. Because everybody knew, that Mad Brad doesn't forgive.

III

2019

A WISE MONKEY, KNOWS WHAT TREE TO CLIMB

Pick your battles carefully

KANO

Kano and a few of his half siblings were on their way to visit their father, over in HMP Parkhurst, on the Isle of Wight. It had been over ten years since Bradley had been sent down on a murder conviction but their father's reputation, was still alive on the streets of London and further afield. Bradley had influence both inside and outside of the prison walls and his drugs were supplying many people back in London - and not just the South of the capital, these days - as well as strengthening bonds with big time wholesale buyers and sellers, from up and down the country. That kind of influence automatically fell down to Bradley's offspring; they were respected just because of who they were. Because of who their father was. People didn't mess with them because everyone knew all about, Mad Brad and just because he was locked up, that didn't mean that Bradley Brown, couldn't get to you. Kano knew that his father had been the reason that several people had disappeared, or had been seriously wounded, because his father had paid for it to happen. Not Joseph, though; that guy had outsmarted Bradley so far, and Kano was beginning to admire the man for that.

Kano was twenty-one now, and had thought that his father would've let him handle some of his business, on the outside.

As the eldest child, and a son, Kano had been entertaining thoughts of being a roadman, from the day he was old enough to understand, who his father was. Bradley was dead against his kids doing anything that he himself, used to do, and was still doing; selling drugs and making a lot of money. It wasn't just about the money though because Kano and his siblings, were well looked after by their dad. Bradley, even sent money to the baby mother's that still checked up on him. Those that had been *wifed off* and had decided, that they'd needed to cut him out of their lives, didn't get shit from Bradley anymore. And Kano's mum Khloe, was on that list. Khloe had gotten pregnant by another man only two and a half years into Bradley's thirty year life sentence, and Kano had a younger half brother now, from his mother. His stepfather, Michael had been good to him, and Kano respected the way that the man had always treated his mother; showering her with love, respect and commitment. Kano had heard the stories about his own father, denying that he'd impregnated his fourteen year old, mother. And then he hadn't even been any type of father for the first, eleven years of Kano's life. Not until Bradley had gone to jail and had needed favours, coercing Khloe to be a mule and smuggle drugs into the prison for him. Kano had gone to school, boasting that his father was a *badman,* until he'd realised that being a bad man, *wasn't* a good thing.

Kano remembered his mother being terrified - nervous for days -before and after the visits. Bradley had thought, that he could buy his kids and anyone else, whom he fancied, using or taking advantage of. But no amount of money or gifts, could make up for how Bradley had treated Kano's, mother. Bradley had sang his own mother's praises to his children, any time that he could, and Kano really liked his paternal grandmother

Candace, but she had enabled her son's, toxic behaviour. First as a child - Kano had also heard the stories about his father's, crazy behaviour as a young boy - but Candace hadn't even stopped enabling her son, once he'd become a man. A father. She was still enabling the bastard, now. Could his grandmother not see, that her son was just rotten? Look at what he'd done to their grandad, her husband. That poor man. Okay, so Delroy smoked rock, but he didn't trouble anyone apart from Candace and he couldn't do that any more, so drugs were the man's only pleasure. Kano thought that his grandma was secretly glad that her son, his father was locked up, because truth be told, Candace was sniffing lines of cocaine and popping Xanax on a regular basis. With a son like Bradley, who could blame the woman?

Kano knew that if his father ever found out, that it was he - Kano - that was supplying Candace with unprescribed pharmaceuticals and party drugs, whenever he passed by her house on the Battersea Park Estate Estate, his life would be over. But his grandmother was a grown woman and should've been free to make her own decisions. So should Kano for that matter, the young man had resolved. He was fed up of living in his father's shadow without being given the opportunity to shine, to come out of the darkness. If Kano said that he was ready for the road life, then Bradley should've just trusted him and given him a chance to prove himself. Bradley had other youngens running, working for him. It was embarrassing that Kano wasn't on anything. Wasn't allowed to be on anything. It made him look weak, wet; like some dickhead!

Kano was fed up, of just being Mad Brad's, son. He wanted to be Killer Kano, and if his dad still thought that he was just an innocent little kid, then he was going to be in for a shock.

Kano had already started building his own phone line, for cocaine and MDMA for the party goers, away from London. The UK was much bigger than London but there had been no point in Kano trying to do business in another big city like Liverpool, Manchester or Leeds. He hadn't wanted to go that far North anyhow and would never have considered Birmingham, because he just would not have coped with that accent. Kano couldn't 't stand it, at all. In the end he'd gone down to Brighton, because it wasn't too far from London where his friends and associates were, and he'd wanted to stay relatively near to his mum, brother and step dad who now lived in Essex; just a ninety minute drive, via the M25, on a good day.

Another pro about Brighton, had been that it wasn't too white for coastal town - for a black man like himself - if you stayed close to the town centre. It was also busy enough to move about and blend in. He'd met a girl down there, in a club called, Tide. She'd bought a few wraps of coke from him, and had offered to snort some off his *aubergine,* and had done just that, a few minutes later, outside the club, in his car. They'd returned to the club and partied the night away, unable to untangle their arms or tongues. Kano had literally moved in with her that very night and things were going well between them. The bird, Mercedes, was mother to a toddler, whose father wasn't on the scene and Kano was cool with that. He could play the role of the step father, in exchange for a roof over his head, cooked meals and sex whenever he wanted. Obviously he was also contributing to the household bills, but he wasn't yet making big money, so he couldn't splurge. Life was comfortable, though. He had no complaints.

Kano had used money that he'd received from Bradley, to start out his little hustle, but he no longer needed the handouts from his father. He didn't depend on, ask or even expect anything from that man, any more. Of course that didn't stop him from spending the money whenever it did hit his bank account, which was very occasionally now, anyway. Kano believed that, that was the least his father could do, since not being able to work for Bradley or for himself in London, without making his father go crazy, had forced Kano to up sticks. Ironically, Bradley had been encouraging Kano to leave London for a while but the stupid man had thought that it would be for his son to attend university. Kano hadn't even got the grades he'd needed to go to college after his GCSE's but his mother had agreed to lie to his father, just to save him from the inevitable lecture. Anyway, money was money at the end of the day, and Kano would never say no to any paper with the Queens face on it.

Bradley had bought an Audi Q7 for Kano as soon as he'd passed his driving test. Once Kano had turned eighteen and could visit his father without another adult, he'd made the long trip to see Bradley once or twice per month, with some of his younger half siblings. Parkhurst prison was a mission to get to - crossing via ferry from Southampton - but it was the only prison his father would reside in because he had the screws, in his pocket, doing whatever he asked of them and getting him what he wanted and needed. For a price, of course. Kano was cool with all of his younger half-siblings on his father's side but he didn't trust them not to report everything he did, back to Bradley. They had all forgiven Bradley for his earlier years of failing as a father but Kano had not. Kano, just like Bradley, found it very hard to forgive people and he'd soon be leaving the Q7 parked up on Candace's driveway. Kano wouldn't be coming back to visit Bradley after today. This was a goodbye from Kano but Bradley wouldn't even know it.

Everyday you goad the donkey, then one day it will kick you.

Kano had had enough! He couldn't kick his dad physically, although he'd love to. Kano despised the man but there was always a table and plenty of burly prison officers that prevented him from giving his father, exactly what he deserved. Kano was done with Bradley though. He was moving away from London and the watchful eyes of his younger half siblings, as well as all of his father's other spies. Kano was leaving Mad Brad, the Fuck-boy Dad, behind. Just like Bradley had left his mum when she was pregnant. And then abandoned Kano too, for eleven long years. Kano would do his own thing now, since his father didn't want to help him. He didn't need Bradley. Kano would make it on his own. Just watch me, the young fool thought to himself.

SHANE

I've always been a sea air, kind of guy, I just never got enough of it in my life, before I moved here. I like it down here because I can blend in, and I needed to be able to blend in amongst a sea of people and not bring attention to myself. Not stand out too much. There are enough black people in Brighton town centre these days, to avoid being too conspicuous. It was almost as cosmopolitan as London, but the people are friendlier and the I'd always fancied living by the sea. I've been living here long enough to spot the locals from the tourists, smiling and nodding at some of the familiar faces. I used to be a tourist here myself many moons ago but now I live here with my Missus, Julia and our three daughters, Kyla, Keeyley and Khelani. They're my only family now. Both my parents are dead. Neither of them lived to see me, meet and marry my gorgeous, honourable wife. I miss them both dearly. I wish I'd been a better person, a better son, when they were still alive. Given them less stress, stayed off the streets and away from certain types of people. Bradley Brown, in particular. I wish I'd stayed away from the road lifestyle, but here I was, still dealing drugs. That was because there weren't many other options for me; I have poor qualifications and a criminal record that features numerous violent crimes. I have a wife and three children to provide for. What was I expected to do?

My wife is French and from a well-to-do family and they have welcomed me into their lives and homes and I'm very grateful for what I do have now. Grateful for the fact that I'm alive when I know that I shouldn't be. God is good. I would've said that God was great, if He hadn't called my parents home so soon. Family was everything to me and I had spent too many years of my young life, putting others before my parents. My father had died of a heart attack whilst I was still living at home and I know my mother had blamed me in part for that, because I had been the reason that the police had kept using the battering ram on my parents' front door. The reason they had been so stressed out all of the time. I wish I had never been, what my parents had referred to, as an *Area Boy,* a street rat. Then to lose my mother to cancer - to not even know that she'd had a terminal illness - and to not be able to say goodbye, hold her hand, send her off. It had almost killed me.

Then the biggest blow, was seeing Bradley post my mother's funeral pictures on his Facebook account, from his prison cell, with the caption: *We gave auntie Aku a great farewell.* That post had sickened and floored me. I hadn't thought I could hate Bradley any more than I already did, but I knew better after seeing that shit, but still more horror was to follow. One day I thought I'd log into my old email and there in my inbox, were videos of my baby mothers, using dildos, climaxing and calling out Bradley's name. Both of them. Together in the same room, sitting on the same bed. I'd known that those cousins were weird and fucked up but that hadn't stopped me from nearly throwing up. I did actually vomit when the next video I opened, showed my girls blowing kisses towards the camera, saying we love you Daddy Bradley. The videos were sent back in 2012, when Deja and Tayjah would've been much younger than they'd be now. The daughters that I'd been forced to give up and abandon all those years ago. How fucking dare Bradley?

How I wished I could turn the clock back, so that I could make my parents proud of me, instead of disappointed. I knew now, that everything that they'd told me was true; friends were temporary. The street lifestyle was temporary. It was nothing to be glorified. It was tearing apart communities and leaving children without their fathers and mothers without their sons. I wish I'd worked harder in school and went to the library with the *neeks,* because I bet they would all be feeling safe and unafraid of walking the streets in the area in which they lived, right now. That was no way to live your life. I feel relatively safe now, here in Brighton but I can never completely let my guard down. I didn't want my new family to lose me. They had no clue about my past. I was a different person now and I had wanted to keep my past, in the past. I had just wanted to enjoy my life and to stop living in fear.

* * *

I ended the call and picked up my car keys. I then kissed all four of my girls and said that I'd be back soon with a fish and chip tea and of course, some sweets. I would surprise my wife with some flowers too. Julia was so beautiful and so sweet. She'd turned a blind eye to my dealing because I wasn't selling ten pound *shots,* to junkies; I was moving bigger amounts now and dealing with rich, white and Arab businessmen. It had taken some grovelling and convincing before Julia had relented, having threatened to chuck me out the house and divorce me, until she saw the money. It was all good after that. We live in a nice house, we both drive a Range Rover and we go on at least four family holidays, abroad each year. Our children were at a state primary school for now, but the plan was to send all three girls to a private secondary school and that was going to cost us a lot. Julia and the girls have a great life but there were things that they didn't know about me and I didn't want them to know, but I wasn't sure if I could hide it forever because of what I was about to do.

You see, I'm one step ahead of them. I was ready and I was going to strike first. It was kill or be killed as far as I was concerned and I had no intention of deserting my second family, like I had my first. I'd been forced to abandon my mum, my daughters, my home and my life. I had already let my mother, father and my other two daughters down and had still been blessed with a new family. I wasn't trying to mess up my second chance at life. It would serve as warning; I was a different person now. The fear that I'd lived with for so long had turned from fear for myself into fear for my family. Even if the old rule of *no kids allowed* still applied, and my number one enemy only came after me, my daughters would be absolutely devastated if they lost their father. I had to make sure that I wasn't the one to die. Not today, not tomorrow, not even next year. Not for a good few decades, at least.

I drove the short distance to a secluded dirt track that wasn't covered by CCTV, but was still close enough to the town centre for me to get the things I'd promised my girls and get home without raising any suspicion. If anybody ever came knocking, asking questions about where I'd been on this particular evening and I said that I'd been at home all day, hopefully Julia wouldn't think it was essential to mention my fifteen minute trip to get chocolate, chips and chrysanthemums. Furthermore, Joseph knew his wife would back up his alibi without question. Julia was like that; fiercely supportive and fiercely defensive of me and our girls.

This was a great place to park up and do quick drug deal and I had done just that, right here, many, many times before but today would be different though. I'd been watching this lad around town for a while now. He seemed to be dealing to clientele at the clubs and bars at night - sometimes alone, sometimes with company. I hadn't even been sure at first but then one day I'd heard the name, and when I'd turned around it was like looking straight at someone from my past but this face was much younger. There hadn't been any recognition in the young man's face, as he'd stood behind me and my family with his family, in the amusement arcade. All of us, restlessly waiting in the queue to exchange our tokens for the amusement's dross prizes.

Being well off didn't stop us from doing cheap days out around town. It was important to support local businesses and even though we all know that those amusement arcades are a scam, it made our girls happy and that's all I'd ever wanted for my children. Then and now. Happiness. Safety. Security. I had nearly dropped down dead and saved someone else a job when I'd turned around that day, though. I'd been on even higher alert ever since then and had followed the young man, discreetly for weeks. At first, I had thought my time was up. Then I'd been confused as to why the young man hadn't tried to kill me yet. Once I had realised he was probably just here by coincidence, I made the first move.

I cornered him one night outside of the Tide nightclub and told him that he'd need to buy his product from me if he wanted to continue trading around here. I offered him a good price but I will be giving him more than he's expecting, here today. This was going to be, a different type of transaction. This one was for my mum and dad. I *dey miss you.*

Restless feet might walk you into a snake pit.

Kano's feet were restless and I was the snake, waiting in my pit.

D.I JOHNSON

I've had my eye on my informant for the past ten years. I've long since been promoted up the ranks, and he hasn't operated on my patch for even longer; hasn't provided any intelligence to me or any of my colleagues, since that murder trial all those years ago. He has been doing the same sort of poisonous business, elsewhere, on my Royal, British territory, though, and I'd informed my colleagues down in East Sussex. They had been watching him, too, but not very closely mind, because this man moves with caution, and doesn't flaunt his operation in their faces. He mainly stays out of sight and conducts his business meetings on private premises but just because those beach bum plods, didn't want to ruffle any feathers, that didn't mean that I had to let him carry on breaking the law, untouched and increasing his wealth via the proceeds of those crimes. I was eager to get him off the streets and fate, sent me an assistant to help me achieve that.

At first, I'd thought that the younger man was there, to end the life of the man that I'd never lost track of, for too long, but it turned out to be an unlikely coincidence. And I don't usually believe in those, but the two men had been doing their own thing for a while and not made contact. Until last week, when that changed, and my one-time, informant, approached the other, younger man, and there was what appeared to be, a perfectly, reasonable and civil conversation, between the two men.

That was when I made my decision to intervene and *cause* a reaction. I did think that it was strange, considering that the younger of the two men, looked just like his father. A face that the older of the two scumbags, could never have forgotten. I had followed the younger man from his illegal activities one night, and had waited outside and knocked on his front door, once his girlfriend had left home, the next morning. She had been with whom I had assumed, was their preschool-aged, son. I had shown the boy my warrant card, when he'd answered my knock, and asked if I could enter his abode, just so that we could talk. When he looked worried, I had reassured him, that I was there to *help* him and not to arrest him. The boy had been compliant and had pulled back the front door further, permitting me to enter his home. The smell of cannabis, had immediately attacked my nostrils, and the boy had become, instantly, evidently, terrified.

"I don't care about a bit of weed", I had told him, when the smell of his nervousness, had overpowered the smell of the class B drug. Once seated inside his home, I'd explained to him, that I knew exactly who he was, because I knew his father. I had also told him, that I knew the guy, I'd seen him talking to outside the Tide nightclub, the previous night. I had disclosed to the fool, that I knew he was a small-time cocaine and MDMA dealer, and that it was his father's arch enemy, Joseph Aku, who I wanted to capture.

I had generously and regrettably, offered Kano a way out; I would tell my colleagues down in Brighton to give him a wide berth, after all, he was just selling small amounts of cocaine, and

MDMA to party goers. Shane on the other hand was selling and buying drugs by the kilo, living a very comfortable life from the proceeds of crime, and that's what the police don't like to see. Why should I work my arse off to afford occasional luxury whilst others do barely anything, except poison our environment and our communities but yet still, they live better than the rest of us? Better than us, *law abiding* citizens.

Once I had revealed to Kano, that the man outside the club was his father's old, friend-turned-enemy, Joseph Aku, I could tell without a doubt, that the shock denoted by the lad's facial expression, was genuine. Shane had had work done on his face - paid for by himself, not the Home Office - and he did not look like Joseph any more, but he could not hide from the police. I had never let him out of my sight and I knew the name and location of his plastic surgeon. Shane may have thought that he was clever, but he was just as stupid as the man, he had been running from, for so long.

Kano really hadn't had a clue that he'd crossed paths - several times too over the past eighteen months - with Joseph Aku, and it was stimulating for me, to be the one to make him aware of that fact. All the idiot had to do, was arrange a meeting with Shane, to buy a significant amount of cocaine and I had planned to be present, when the Brighton boys in blue, nabbed him. After all, it was me that was assisting them, to reel in a big, score. If we - they - could catch Shane with a wholesale amount of cocaine, it would be a very straightforward conviction; *bang to rights*. I knew very well that young Kano didn't have the kind of money that he needed to buy that much of the stuff, but his father certainly did, and I had been hoping to entrap Bradley Brown, without either the father or son, figuring out, what I was up to.

Bradley had been serving drugs as well as time and he piece of shit, had been benefiting from what was designed to be a punishment. It was ludicrous and fucking embarrassing for the common, loyal and patriotic, Englishman. I was about to complete my thirty years of serving in the Force and I wanted to go out with a bang, and I'd figured, that utilising these black bastards, was the way to achieve that. I was a Detective Inspector now. My powers reached much further, than they used to.

I was definitely going to go out with a bang but it was even more spectacular than I could've imagined.

Opportunities don't just happen, you have to create them.

Sometimes, police work is less traditional and we have to move things along. *They* will try to call it a set up, but really, they set themselves up. They honestly, just make it way too easy for me.

BRADLEY

Bradley was worried about Kano. He'd barely been to visit him these past twelve months and Bradley was starting to believe that his eldest son was getting too big for his boots. He'd soon be advising Kano, that he needed to listen to the song by Stormzy of the same title. The boy obviously needed a reminder and that was the friendliest message that his father could offer. A slap around his fucking head, wouldn't be far behind depending on Kano's response.

Kano didn't understand that his father was simply trying to protect him. Trying to keep him away from prison and to ensure that Kano and all of his other children, lived a better life than he had. Why was that such a bad thing? Bradley provided for all of his offspring now, even the older ones like Kano, who was a grown arse adult. The monthly allowance should've been more than enough but some people were just ungrateful and among all the things that Bradley couldn't stand, the ingratitude of those that he'd helped was near the top. He wasn't obligated to give Kano a penny of his own money now that the boy was over eighteen years of age but Bradley had recognised, that he had plenty of years to make up for and he'd been trying to do so but the way Kano was behaving, was really pissing him off.

Son or no son, Kano would need putting in his place very

soon, if he didn't fix up his attitude and remember who the fuck Bradley was. Not just as the young man's father but as an O.G. Kano may have had the notion that his father couldn't do anything from behind bars, but Bradley knew he could order his son's death easily, if he chose to. Kano was only untouchable because of who his father was. The boy had better remember that and start acting accordingly, if he didn't want to be on the receiving end of his father's anger. No kids allowed didn't apply to nineteen year old men and Bradley was fast losing patience with his entitled gen Z son. Maybe he needed to stop the lad's hand outs altogether, let Kano see how hard life would be without his father's assistance and protection.

Bradley had been providing security for his son down in Brighton ever since the boy had started moonlighting in the clubs at weekends; even before Kano had relocated permanently to that part of the country. He'd had people keeping an eye out for Kano and the bird he was now, shacked up with. Bradley knew that the kid wasn't Kano's son and Bradley didn't want his money going on Kano's step sprog, so he'd been sending the boy less bread recently anyway. Too many people had turned their back on Bradley over the past ten years and he was fed up of people treating him like a nobody. Especially, his own fucking son!

The older the moon, the brighter the shine.

Kano needed to start respecting his elders and to remember that his father knows best. The boy was going to end up in serious trouble with the law or with the type of scumbags that people are forced to associate with in the criminal world. Kano was out of his depth but his father knew that the boy would soon learn that the hard way if he refused to tow the line. There really wasn't much more that Bradley could do to protect Kano from where he was but he had always been looking out for the boy, his son just didn't know it.

And Bradley knew that his stubborn son wouldn't have been grateful if he'd found out, so his men knew to stay well hidden. They hadn't yet found Joseph, so Bradley's faith in their abilities wasn't as strong as it had once been but who knew what Kano would get up to, if he was left totally unsupervised. It wouldn't be long before Bradley would find that out, and he would realise that he'd had every reason, to be worried.

KANO

Kano hadn't believed it when the policeman had told him, that the guy who'd accosted him outside the nightclub, had been the one and only Joseph Aku. The man responsible for putting his dad behind bars. The same man that his father has had people hunting down without success, for the past ten years. Kano wasn't a snitch but he'd wanted to know what the police knew about his own dealing and he was glad that he'd let the copper into his girlfriend's flat and heard what he'd had to say. He had done what the copper had asked of him and he'd contacted Joseph to arrange a meet to purchase some cocaine, but Kano wasn't actually going to follow through with what the policeman had hoped for.

Kano needed time to think and plan his next move. He needed to consult with his father. The man he'd been shunning for the past year or so. It had been a while but this was huge news. Once the copper had left him, Kano texted Shane.

SUMTHING CAME UP
CNT MEET 2DAY
WILL RAINCHK

Kano was definitely expecting to play with the big boys now

but he was playing with fire.

Hang your basket, where you can reach it.

Kano hadn't yet received the lesson from the universe about biting off more than he could chew, but the lesson was on it's way.

SHANE

Abeg! The stupid prick cancelled the meet. He'd wasted my time but I wasn't worried, just pissed off. Killer Kano, as he's known on the streets and in the clubs around here, was not going to be killing me. I was confident that the boy did not know who I was, so my family and I were safe. It was Kano that should've been worried. And his father, that dickhead, Bradley. Bradley was doing big things, I knew that from his social media and his reputation; even in Brighton, the name Mad Brad resonated. I was well aware that because Bradley's power and money stretched so far, had I not been able to pay for plastic surgery to change the way I looked, I would've been dead long before my mother. And all of this hassle for all of these years, when those stupid bitches hadn't even given me my full share of the cocaine that *they'd* stolen from Bradley. I had planned the whole thing with both of my baby mother's, who are actually first cousins. As they were both wearing black tracksuits and balaclavas, Bradley had just assumed that the two figures that he'd seen rob us - well, rob him - were male. If it hadn't been for the profits I had skimmed, scammed and stashed away over the years, without Bradley noticing or saying anything about it at the time, I'd never have been able to afford the reconstructive surgery and would not have been able to stay so well hidden.

Those two bitches, whom I'd reproduced with, were all cosy with Bradley to this day, writing messages about missing him on Facebook, frequently. If Bradley had known that it had been Shanelle and Sharlene that had robbed him, they'd both be dead and my daughter's would've lost their mother's, so I had never intended to reveal the truth to Bradley. Since Kano didn't know who I was, I had the upper hand and I was going to be playing it, sooner rather than later. This game was drawing to an end, now. It was time to leave my past, truly in my past but there was just one last thing, that I had to do first.

A chattering bird, builds no nest.

I was past talking to Kano, now. Bradley was fully responsible for what I was soon, going to do. This was going to be for my parents and my two girl's, whom he'd taken and made his own, with Deja and Tayjah often posting on their 'Dad', Bradley's Facebook page. As much as it hurt, they seemed happy so after this was done, I would rest and enjoy a happy life, too. Comfortably, with my new and treasured family. I had lost two daughters but gained three more and a wife. I was a happy man.

If only Bradley had chosen peace, this wouldn't have had to happen. But Mad Brad loved problems more than he appreciated peace and now I was going to give him a big fucking problem. A get back of my own, for what Joseph had lost and Bradley wouldn't even know that it was from me. I would ensure that I kept the life that I had created for myself, here. A life that I loved and would do absolutely anything to protect. No matter how much money Bradley Brown may have had, he'd never know the happiness that I felt now, have felt ever since I met Julia. Bradley would never know true love because he didn't have it in him. He couldn't know love, with all that hate in his heart. It was a shame that young Kano was going to pay for his father's mistakes but that was going to be Bradley's problem, not mine.

BRADLEY

Bradley was pumped up. His boy Kano, his own flesh and blood and his eldest child, had the *drop* - the location - on that dickhead, Joseph Aku. Ten long years and a lot of man power and no one had managed to find him, until now. And Bradley couldn't have asked for a better result; his own son was the winner of the one hundred thousand pound cash reward. Bradley wasn't planning on handing over all of that, though; he'd never been serious about the cost of the bounty. He'd just thought that the job would've been done years ago, with that kind of monetary incentive. Better late than never, though, had always been Bradley's attitude, in regards to getting his, *get back*. There was no expiration date for vengeance as far as Bradley was concerned.

Bradley could've waited, the full thirty years if he'd had to but he was glad that he wouldn't need to, now. Joseph had been on the run for far too long already. It was another violation; that he'd mugged Bradley off for so long. It was embarrassing for Bradley and his associates but nobody had ever been stupid enough, to mock Bradley for his failure to catch that pussy, after all, he was locked up. He had been reliant upon the muppets on the outside, men whom he'd thought would've had, some power and loyalty to offer him, but they had failed the mission.

Bradley had never wanted Kano to get involved in this life. And he still didn't. The life Bradley had lived and was still living, was dangerous. Kano hadn't elaborated on how he'd got the information about Joseph but Bradley knew where his son was, even if Kano wasn't aware of that, and that meant that he also knew where Joseph Aku was likely to be. Kano had been so eager to be involved in the street life, that Bradley knew that his son would've probably gone all out, and exhausted all avenues, just to try and impress him and get his foot in the door of the dangerous, criminal lifestyle that his father was trying to shield him from. Kano was out to try and prove, that he should be out in the *fields,* making *moves* and getting his hands dirty with violence and drugs, but it was all starting to make sense now.

Kano had revealed one important piece of information; the reason that Joseph had been so illusive, for such a long time, was because he'd had reconstructive work done on his face. There was one big problem though; Kano looked very much like Bradley, so Joseph would definitely have recognised him but Kano had insisted that the two men, had not yet been acquainted; apparently, they had never been in close proximity. Bradley had warned his son, to make sure that it stayed that way. Kano couldn't be too careful out there, and even though the boy may have thought that he knew everything, Bradley knew better. Bradley knew that his eldest child, really didn't know much about anything at all. He was empty upstairs - no braincells - hence so eager to live a life that was not even necessary for him to live.

Bradley had come from nothing. Yes, his mother had always worked a good job and given him a comfortable enough life, but she'd still had to worry about not being able to pay a bill, some months. She'd sometimes had to sacrifice something for herself, in order to give Bradley what he'd wanted, on top of everything that a child needs, and she did it with ease, without any assistance from Delroy. Bradley didn't want to be like his dad and he'd been trying to be a good father for the past ten years but Kano treated him with the same disdain that he felt towards Delroy. That was painful because in Bradley's own eyes, he'd been a much better father to his children, than Delroy had ever been to him.

Bradley believed that he had now done enough for Kano, to deserve the boy's respect and not receiving it, had given him restless nights, heart palpitations and recurrent dreams of suffocating the ungrateful, little shit with a pillow. Kano still hadn't seemed to notice, that he himself was being watched, down in Brighton. Bradley wondered how his own surveillance hadn't identified Joseph, before remembering again, that the the snake had changed his whole face. Bradley had told Kano to hold tight; not to do anything until his father had gotten back to him. Bradley just hoped that his hard-ears child, would actually listen and do as he'd been told for once because Bradley did not trust Joseph Aku. The guy was the biggest snake that he'd ever come across.

Joseph had stolen from Bradley, set him up to receive a life sentence, and then managed to evade capture himself, for a whole fucking decade. Bradley didn't know much about cosmetic surgery but he knew that a whole new face, wasn't cheap. He also knew that D.S Johnson, who had now been promoted to a Detective Inspector, would not have gone out of his way to ensure that the prosecution's star witness in his case - the case that had put Bradley where he was right now – had a comfortable new start by the English coast, a brand new face and whole new fucking identity. Bradley knew that sort of service wasn't given to people like Joseph. Instead they were convinced to inform on their acquaintances - to stand up and be a witness in court - and then once the case was over, they were more or less, left to your own devices. Some of them murdered or seriously injured as a result of snitching but people like Joseph, still risked their lives to do it anyway and now Joseph's comeuppance was about to be served.

This new information, confirmed to Bradley, that Joseph must've been stealing from him, for a long while, to have afforded his new look. It would soon prove to have been a waste of time and money, because it will be buried six feet under. Bradley couldn't help smiling to himself but Joseph was definitely cunning and sly and he should not be underestimated. Bradley was scared that Kano would make that mistake, whilst also praying that his son actually took his advice for once, and did absolutely *nothing*.

A pound of fret, couldn't pay an ounce of debt.

Bradley knew it was pointless worrying about the situation, but that didn't stop him from doing so because Kano was a loose cannon. The boy was stupid and unpredictable. Bradley was well aware – having often been pissed off by it - that the boy found following his instructions, extremely difficult, almost to the point of *impossible*. All Bradley could do was hope and make Dua, that everything would work out for the best.

KANO

The young man was feeling cocky and confident. He had parked up and waited a short distance from the Tide club, certain that Joseph or whatever he was called these days, would go looking for him. Not just today. He'd come looking for him a few nights already this week, without any sign of the snitch. The idea had been to follow the dude back to his own car, then his home, to try to reason with the guy. The man had called him plenty of times in the weeks that had passed since Kano had cancelled the meet up between them but Kano had needed to do this in person, so he had aired all the calls and messages. He had also been airing the calls from his father and the policeman, too. Kano was only answering calls on the number, that neither of those men had.

Tonight though, Joseph *had* come to the Tide and now the younger of the two men, was going to present himself but on his terms. Kano had planned on appealing to Joseph's businessman persona before making the snitch aware of who he was speaking to; the eldest son of his biggest *opp*. Kano had thought that it was going to be easy because he was offering the man a chance to carry on living, the alternative being that Kano could've just killed him, right then and there.

Bradley had told his son to sit tight and do nothing and that had helped Kano make up his mind to do *something*. Anything. He wasn't as stupid as his father thought he was; Kano knew that his father would get somebody else to deal with Joseph, pay them a lot less than the hundred thousand pounds, that had been on offer for ten long years, and hadn't even increased in line with inflation. Bradley would've ended up just *gifting* Kano whatever he'd felt like giving him, and then Kano would've remained in the exact same position that he was in , now. Level zero. Well, Joseph seemed to be doing very well for himself and the man was definitely clever. A snitch yes, but nobody could deny that Joseph Aku, had out smarted *everyone,* including Bradley, by evading capture and was living freely. Unlike Kano's stupid father, who still had twenty years to serve behind bars. Kano knew whose team he'd prefer to be on.

Loyalty came at a cost and Bradley had been too cheap to afford the loyalty of his own son. Kano had bought himself an Audi Q5, after leaving the Q7 that his father had bought him, on Candace's drive. She'd been upset to hear that Kano was moving down to Brighton permanently, but that was probably more to do with the fact that he wouldn't be able to supply her with her vices as often as he had been.

Kano was enjoying all this cloak and dagger stuff, thinking that he was good at being discreet, even entertaining thoughts that maybe he could work for MI5 if the drug dealer and street lifestyle didn't work out for him. He had followed Joseph back from the club undetected, on the semi-busy streets of Brighton on a Thursday night. When the man that his father loathed and wanted dead, turned into a side street up ahead of him - just a short drive from the sea front - Kano had felt positive that his plan was going to be successful. He now knew who Shane really was and he'd soon know where the man lives. Where his children live. Kano now recognised Shane; he'd seen him a few times, around the pier and the promenade.

Kano hadn't planned on delivering a direct threat to the older man, he was just going to drop a few hints to the guy; let him know that he could and *should* kill him, but that he wasn't his father's *send-out* boy. Kano would tell the snitch that he'd prefer to do some business with him instead. He'd apologise for not turning up, to meet him previously, and shake the man's hand with a firm grip. He would show Shane - if that's that he preferred to be called these days - that he *was,* a big man. Kano truly believed that the guy could only be grateful to him, for sparing his life. But Kano should've listened to his father because Kano, as was his default setting, was wrong.

Who doesn't hear, must feel.

Kano was his own worst enemy, and would've done well if he'd just done as his father had advised, instead of trying to emulate his father's life. Bradley Brown was a lot of things but apart from letting his mum handle the proceeds of his criminality, to prevent it being confiscated by the police, he didn't get his family involved in his business. It was for their own good. Kano should've understood and accepted that, but instead he was going to walk straight into the lion's den.

SHANE

The silly boy probably thought that he'd been so clever, but he would've been very wrong about that. Kano couldn't tail someone covertly, if his life had depended on it. And it did. I'd gone searching for him, to ask about him not turning up and then ignoring my calls ever since but he'd been nowhere to be found at the Tide or PRYZM. It didn't take long for the fool to show up though - in my rear view mirror. When you've been dodging a one hundred thousand pound bounty on your head for ten years, you become adept at observing your surroundings. The apple hadn't fallen far from the tree though, with Kano being as stupid as his father but that was about to go in my favour.

This message was going to be delivered from Joseph, though, not Shane. It didn't matter that Bradley wouldn't know who the message was from. I would know. I would feel like some justice had been served for everything that I've lost. The only thing I still had from my roots, was my family name; I'd remained an Aku, changing only my given name from Joseph to Shane. I had even had my face reconstructed to hide my West African roots. I had sworn all those years ago, that I'd get back at Bradley if anything happened to my mother before it was safe for me to return home, and it was now time to keep that promise.

Once I'd noticed Kano following me, I decided that I was not going to change my destination. I continued to drive to a rental property in an area of lots of other rental properties. It was a three bedroom detached house, with a long, winding driveway. Tall, towering trees, lined both sides of the drive, their leaves bending forward at the top, creating a natural archway. Julia, who'd been the one to secure this property, had called it magical, having viewed it without me because the landlord's around these parts, were more inclined to let to white tenants. And that didn't always extend to white tenants, with black partners or black children. Once Julia had signed the lease and taken me to see it in person for the first time, all I had seen were trees that offered me a complete blanket of privacy.

"Nothing magical here", I'd said, before Julia had started walking down the drive towards the house, discarding a piece of her clothing, one by one, as she strutted expertly in her heels. She had stripped down to her underwear, and then proceeded to get totally, naked. Except for her patent So Kate Louboutin's; bending over, with her legs parted at the entrance to the house. The extra privacy had been well and truly appreciated on that day and on many others since then. We had definitely taken advantage of the fact that most of the neighbouring homes were mostly used for stag and hen weekenders; spaced far enough apart, and well insulated, so that you'd not to be bothered by the raucous crowds, in any building that you weren't inside of. Not that any noise would effect me much, since I was never there for more than a few hours at a time. Apart from when Julia gets all erotic and wants to come and have sex up against the tall wide, unadorned upstairs windows.

My wife definitely knew how to keep the fire ablaze between us. Having got pregnant three years in a row with our daughters,

I'd had mates and *colleagues,* who'd assumed that I'd missed out on lots of sex during that period but how wrong they were. Julia wanted sex all day, everyday and *anywhere* and for her, pregnancy didn't change that. If anything, she wanted even more sex. I'm not ashamed to admit, the woman tired me out. I needed caffeine and cocaine to keep up the performance but I would do anything for my wife. She deserves, everything great in life and it's my duty to ensure that she receives that.

Nowhere was out of bounds for Julia. She was a very daring and very sexy lady. We'd entered the mile high club on a business flight to Paris before travelling on to Cap d'Agde after our scheduled meetings, simply to have public sex on its naturist beach. We'd experienced dogging down at Devil's Dyke in Brighton and Julia had even given me oral pleasure, in her hospital suite, after each of our daughters were born. She hadn't even stopped when the nurse had walked in and caught her at it, after our second daughter Keeyley was born. It had then become a joke amongst the midwives, when Julia had our third and final daughter; instead of being embarrassed, after Khelani was born, Julia had told the midwives, to *knock the fucking door please, because I'm about to give my hubby a spit and shine.*

Even Julia's parents seemed to know about their daughters lust and addiction to orgasms and always gave us the bedroom at the very top of their French villa, whenever we were all out there together. They had even made jokes about still needing earplugs to block out their only child's, cries at night. Sometimes I'd be so nervous around my in-laws, knowing that Julia could be sexually inappropriate at any time, but the French were definitely more liberal than Nigerians. My parents would have beat the both of us and banned us from their home, if we'd done anything but hold hands under their roof. We wouldn't have been able to be intimate in our *own* home, if they were present, much less.

It was ironic that Killer Kano was going to be killed at an Airbnb that I'd been using as a stash house, considering how this shit all started. I sped up to widen the gap between my Range Rover and his Audi Q5, whilst still making sure that he wouldn't lose me. I indicated to signify where I was going - left down a private road that leads to the holiday rental home - then once I'd made the turn, I drove even faster knowing it was a dead end, and Kano was 200 metres behind me. About one hundred metres down the private road, I operated a remote gate that was camouflaged as a bush and drove through it. Kano would not even notice this additional entrance and exit to the property; the gate really looked like a bush, when closed. It was another feature that had caught Julia's eye when she had been checking out properties for me to conduct my business from. Nothing illegal ever entered our family home.

The plan was for Kano to continue on up the private road that I'd just been on, and I would greet him at the front door, having entered the house from the front. And then it would be lights out for the kid. I started to worry that Kano would just turn around and drive away when he didn't see my car on the drive, but I was hoping that the boy was curious and stupid enough to approach the house. This house was grand and worth over a million pounds. Anybody would want to take a closer look. As I entered the house through the back door, locking it again and walking through the kitchen towards the hall, and front door, I heard the sound of a car getting nearer and I smiled, at what was about to happen.

I'd already made prior arrangements, weeks ago, with some

Albanian guys that I do business with, in preparation for what I was going to do. For the amount that I'd paid them, I was confident that they'd do an immaculate clean up job, and leave no forensic evidence. I stood at the front door and looked through the peephole. Kano parked his car and got out, and even from a distance, it was like seeing Bradley at that age. The days, when the two of us were still friends. Kano was definitely his father's twin; the boy had his dad's face and arrogance but if he'd had his father's heart, I'd have been dead already. The fool was looking so cocksure, that it helped to ease my guilt. My conscience; I wasn't going to lose too much sleep, over this idiot. As he got closer, I began to open the front door with my left hand, whilst holding the cold piece of metal that was tucked into the back of my waistband, with my right. I through back the door, and pointed the barrel right at him, but before I could put pressure on the trigger and blast Kano's life away, there was the sound of rustling, high up in those canopying trees, and then what sounded like, semi automatic gunshots. A sound that I had heard before, as the old version of me. As Joseph. Branches begin to snap, and then it seemed like there were people falling from those trees. One person, then another. The sounds of screams or sirens, or maybe both. I feel something hit my chest, and see a red spot, in front of me, Kano is falling. I realise that Kano has been shot. But not by me. I'm still holding my weapon but it hasn't been fired. Not tonight anyway. It's Kano's blood that has splattered onto me and I smile as he hits the concrete, relieved rather than disappointed, that I wasn't the one that killed him. His blood has still ended up on my hands though, with me being so close to him as he was shot. I have no idea who fired those shots but I'm not going to stick around and find out. This has all taken place in about, five seconds and for most of that time, I was stood, rooted to the spot. My fight or flight sensors, were not activating, but I was now over the shock, and I'm fully aware, that I'm in danger, so I go to slam the front door but my legs stop working and I fall to the ground, still in the open doorway. It wasn't Kano's blood that had stained my skin and my clothes. It was my own. I'd been hit by a bullet too. I can hear shouting now: *armed police, lay on the floor and show your hands.*

A person is a person because of other people.

Bradley Brown was the reason for all of this. He had ruined my life. He had hunted me. He had put a price on my head. He was the reason that my mother had died of cancer, alone. I had become who I was, and planned to take Kano's life because of Bradley Brown, but that wasn't going to be of any comfort to my distraught, wife and kids, when they received the news, that I was dead.

IV

2020

BEND THE TREE WHEN IT'S YOUNG, BECAUSE WHEN IT'S OLD, IT WILL BREAK

It's easier to teach children when they are young, than when they are older

BRADLEY

It had been a hard blow, a devastating shock to his system, finding out that his eldest child, was dead. Killed accidentally in the shower of bullets, that had only been intend for one man. Joseph Aku. The fact that Joseph, was in possession of a loaded handgun at the time of his execution, was a definite indication to Bradley, that his son would've died that night, regardless. If Joseph had had that same energy for their opps back in the day, he would've made a better business partner but now Joseph and Kano were both dead and it was a bittersweet feeling for Bradley.

Joseph's baby mother's had come clean to him about their part in the stash house robbery, whilst Bradley was on remand for murder, all the way back, in 2009. Bradley had wanted to slap the both of them, hard across their faces, and not just with his dick, like they had been used to. Their saving grace, had been that they'd still been in possession of most of the cocaine at the time. They had only given a small amount of the half kilo to Joseph, because he had threatened to tell Bradley about their involvement, in the act of disloyalty, but once Bradley was arrested and remanded in prison, Shanelle and Sharlene had come clean to Bradley, in a joint, handwritten letter. Those two cousins were so close, that Bradley had bedded both of them, at the same time, on many occasions, both before and after Joseph had impregnated them. They were not the kind of women, that Bradley would've accepted as his baby mother, but Joseph was the kind of man, that'd had to take whatever he could get. All the same, the throupleship between Bradley and those bitches, had worked for him, throughout his current sentence.

Shanelle and Sharlene had been solid throughout Bradley's current bid, and he had made the most of their well-deserved, gratitude. Bradley had adopted Joseph's daughter's - whom he was Godfather to anyway - as his own. Bradley felt blessed that both girls, loved him back as though, he was their *real* father. Nobody could replace Kano but Bradley knew in his mind and heart, that he had won the *Brown Vs Aku* war; he may have lost a son, but Bradley had also gained two daughters. And two devoted, women. Women who had owed him a favour, for trying to take him for a fool, along with their *wasteman* of a baby father, all those years ago. Women who were now, also dead; killed by Sussex Police, who just so happened to catch wind of their murderous plan. That had never been Bradley's way before, but he had been trying to take out two birds with one stone. He just hadn't been able to bring himself, to be the one to have Shanelle and Sharlene, killed. Having them arrested after killing Joseph, had seemed like the best option available to Bradley, at the time. They weren't meant to die but the police could have those bodies, especially since the bitches had killed his son. Accident or not, they'd have needed to die anyway. Bradley gave a fuck about those two hoes, now he was the only parent that Deja and Tayjah, had left.

The teenagers couldn't stand their mothers much anyway; Bradley had already succeeded in, poisoning the young girls against both of their parents, as well as buying their love and loyalty over the years. Bradley had slowly, and subtly, erased and replaced Joseph's place, in his daughters' lives, but killing their mothers, would've changed the way that the girls viewed him, and Bradley was ultimately trying to be, more Dad Brad, than Mad Brad these days. He couldn't have anticipated that his son would be killed, having been caught in the crossfire. Why was Kano even there?

Bradley, had had people stationed in Brighton, keeping an eye on Kano for a long while. Even though, the men were from London too, they hadn't been from the same area of south London as him. Most of the boys he'd grown up with, had been dead or locked up just like him, for many years but it was only after Bradley had sent an old associate down to Brighton, after he'd served time for the manslaughter of a love rival, that Bradley had received the news, that D.I Thompson seemed to be tailing Kano, too.

Bradley had almost had a heart attack when he'd heard that news. Thompson, Kano and Joseph, in the same British, seaside town? It hadn't make sense and Bradley had been worried that his son was doing the unthinkable, and working with Thompson; being an informant. Bradley would definitely have disowned his son, for that. The police had since confirmed, that Kano, did not have any weapons on his person or in his vehicle, on the night that he was shot and killed, by those dumb bitches with terrible aim and poor eyesight. Bradley doesn't know why his boy was at that rental property, with Joseph and he'd concluded, that he didn't want to know, either. Bradley would even go as far as saying, that maybe it was better that his son *was* dead. Since the details had started to filter out from the investigation - meagrely - Bradley had realised, that the conversations that he'd have needed to have with Kano - if the boy was still alive - would've been extremely hard.

Shanelle and Sharlene had still been firing shots from their positions up in the tree branches, when the armed police had sped up the winding drive to Joseph's Airbnb. Bradley didn't agree with snitching but he could never have ordered the deaths of those two women and looked Deja and Tayjah in the eyes. Bradley had resorted to doing, the *unthinkable*. He'd offered the women, ten thousand pounds each, to shoot Joseph and then he'd informed the police, of *their* murderous plan. That had been the easy part. They'd both jumped to attention and agreed, almost immediately. It was always going to be harder, for Bradley to try and find out, exactly who and where Joseph was, since nobody knew what he looked like now, as a result of the plastic surgery. With D.I Thompson tailing his son, Bradley had recognised, that he had a valid reason to reach out to the police. He hadn't wanted to, but it was a necessary evil.

D.I Thompson had always been a greedy, pig. He would do almost anything for the right price back in the day, and it had been no different when Bradley had contacted him with an offer; reveal the identity of Joseph and the location of where he might be found. The twenty thousand pounds, that the cousins had believed that they would receive for killing Aku, had actually been transferred to the dirty, copper's bank account, long before they'd even arrived in Brighton from Battersea and completed, the assignment. Within fifteen minutes of it leaving an account in Bradley's own name - not his mother, Candace's - he'd received the address of a rental property in Brighton. Along with a recent photograph of the new Joseph, or rather, Shane Aku. Bradley had passed the information on to his men down in Brighton and they had watched the property for a week; tailing Shane and making note that he had ended his work days, by visiting the house that was down the long drive, with the arching trees. He'd be there for anything, from a few minutes to a couple of hours, before leaving and going home to this family for the night. Thompson had been able to retire in a hail of bullets, commendations and a corrupted, backhanded bonus to top up his pension.

Sussex Police weren't at all happy about the four dead bodies in their jurisdiction - especially since two of the dead bodies were a result of police ammunition and all four bodies were black. It was the kind of case that stirs up protests and looting. It was not an *incident* that the powers that be, didn't want blowing up in the media and they had succeeded, because Bradley could only get details from his solicitor. You could barely find a mention via a Google search, and it was presented as a love affair gone wrong. The police and Brighton and Hove City Council, were trying to suppress the information to prevent a panic amongst the locals, as well as a tourism and travel crisis. The deaths of two black drug dealers, originally from London, wasn't that important compared to the amount of revenue that the coastal town stood to lose, if the red tops ran the story. The Daily Mail - or Daily Fail as it was commonly known - would've only focused on the race of the victim's and suspects, giving rise to a moral panic of black people and criminality. The British police were actively trying to avoid being a part of that particular racist, agenda. Or at least pretend to the public, that they were.

Bradley, was of course hurt and grieving for the loss of his son, but Kano should never have been there. All the same, Bradley was holding D.I Thompson partly responsible for his son's death. Thompson had played Kano; the filthy pig, had tried to use Bradley's son as bait and that had backfired, terribly.

Not for Thompson, though. The result had been exactly what Thompson would have wanted, maybe had even facilitated. The only consolation for Bradley, was finding out that Kano *wasn't* a snitch. It wasn't in the boys blood to stoop that low. Bradley laughed now at the irony, that he had snitched on the two women who had killed his son, and his greatest enemy. Joseph and those two hoes were the cause of all of this. It had been *their* actions, that had set off the chain of events that had effected and ended, so many lives.

Bradley hadn't even been granted permission to attend his son's funeral. Khloe was holding him responsible for their child's death and for once, Bradley was in agreement with that bitch. But Kano had also been a spoilt brat and as Bradley's grandmother used to say: ***Rock stone on the river bottom, doesn't know that the sun is hot.***

Kano had lived a very comfortable life. So comfortable, that the boy hadn't known what real fear and danger, were. But Bradley didn't care how spoilt Kano had been, he had been his *son*. His first born. Kano may have been an ungrateful fool, but he'd been Bradley's ungrateful fool and that had to stand for something. Kano's death would not go unpunished.

A Duppy knows who to frighten.

It would seem that Joseph had planned on taking the life of a vulnerable young lad, who hadn't had any knowledge or experience of the *roadman* lifestyle, but Joseph was finally where Bradley wanted him. Six feet under and nothing but a distant memory to those that had once known him. Killed by a bullet, that had travelled straight through his heart. That was the killer shot but Joseph had been a gloopy, bloodied mess, of a lot of holes by the time he'd been zipped into a body bag and transferred to a sterile environment, to undergo an autopsy. Bradley had since been in touch with a law firm, that specialised in police misconduct cases, and he'd been told that he had a very strong,winnable case, against D.I Thompson.

All the transactions that had been made between the two men prior to 2019 had been in cash, but the payment Bradley had made for the information on Joseph, had been transferred directly from Bradley to a Mrs. Pauline Thompson's, HSBC account; she was the policeman's wife. Of course it's different if you're snitching on the police. It just is. Bradley was doing this in honour of his first born. His young King, Kano. May he forever rest in peace.

D.I JOHNSON (Rtd)

What those idiots don't understand, is that we, the police, are a much bigger, more powerful gang, than they will *ever* be. We take intelligence and use it to our advantage. I knew exactly, what I'd been doing when I'd approached that wannabe gangster, Kano. He'd been so desperate to emulate his father but he was never going to make it big time in the drug business; that's the reason that he'd never been arrested. A few wraps of cocaine wasn't worth the paperwork for me in London or my colleagues in East Sussex. If he'd been trying the same shit somewhere less cosmopolitan and more rural, the coppers there, might've just been glad to attend to something other, than a cow blocking a lane.

Kano should've stuck to my original plan, to get Shane - or that fucking Joseph Aku as we all now know him to be - on a drug bust. Instead he had tried to pull one over on me, and look how that had ended. It wasn't something I'd be losing any sleep over. Kano was a parasite like all the other men who think crime pays, and his demise should be celebrated and not mourned. Those four dead bodies, were a victory that should've been celebrated and we *did* celebrate, just not publicly. The fact that Joseph Aku was actually killed by police ammunition and not by the guns recovered from the women's dead bodies - two

Glock 17's - was never disclosed. The Sussex police, actually killed three people that night, but that was for us to know and not for the general public, to find out. When I'd received the information about those degenerate women's plan, to kill Aku, I gave enough intel to those with jurisdiction, but I may have got the times muddled up. It wasn't my fault that the police didn't get there in time to prevent loss of life. Instead they arrived to a shoot-out - an assassination - and they'd had no choice but to shoot the two armed bitches, who had already opened fire from up in the trees, shooting and killing Kano as approached the front door of Joseph Aku's Airbnb. Aku was also armed, so all three men were *legally* killed, but the politics of policing was another reason, why I was happy for my career in the Force, to end. I was now retiring from the Met, with my pension in tact, and I was leaving this shithole and the vermin that roam it, far behind. London with all its *colour* and lawlessness, could perish for all I cared, just as long as it waited until my family and I, had evacuated.

Our home has already been sold and we are all packed up and ready to leave. We'd never have afforded it, if I hadn't taken bribes over the course of my, glittering career. It had all been for a good cause; everyone wants the best for their family. Why should a copper be any different? With the economic pressure that was a result of Brexit and the Covid pandemic, I had needed every extra penny that I had squirrelled away over the years, and I was extremely grateful to all of the criminals, who had made my family's, imminent escape from London, possible but they could all burn in hell, now that they'd served their purpose.

No Black's. No dogs. No Irish.

Those were better days and I was off to pastures new, where at least the blacks, would be a rarer site than I have had to endure for my life's duration, thus far. Goodbye lawless London and the good old Metropolitan Police. It had been fun, but neither of them would be missed by me.

I was sat in my favourite armchair, sipping my scotch and counting down the days till my family and I, finally escaped to a better, more deserved, quality of life. It wasn't long, before I was, unexpectedly and irritatingly, interrupted by the sound of the doorbell. It was after eight at night; the girls were upstairs in their separate bedrooms and Pauline was out having farewell drinks, with some of her close friends and old colleagues. I got up from my comfortable position and went to open the front door, immediately regretting that decision, once I saw who was there, on the other side of my threshold. They were two people whom I recognised; coppers, but not the sort that I respected. These traitors were from the DPS - Directorate of Professional Standards. They *policed* the police, and grassed on their own. Their presence at my front door, had almost, instantaneously, opened up my bowels. Oh my, oh my. I actually wanted to cry. What the fuck had I done? My poor girls. My poor wife. My fucking life. All of it gone, just like that. I'll be facing up to ten years in prison now, with some of the blokes that I've sent there.

"David Thompson, I am arresting you for accepting bribes in public office. You do not have to say anything, but it may harm your defence if you do not mention when questioned, something which you later rely on in court. Anything you do say may be given in evidence. Do you understand?"

Oh I fucking understood, alright. I was finished.

DENOUEMENT

Bradley had a solid alibi for Shane's murder, seen as though he was still incarcerated in HMP Parkhurst, on the Isle of Wight at the time, but *everyone* knew, that it was Bradley Brown, who'd ordered Shane Aku's murder. There just wasn't any *proof* but Bradley, had as good as pulled the trigger, in Julia's narrative. His son being there without a weapon, had muddied the water and left more questions than answers for the police. And Julia, because she had been carrying out her own investigation. She'd been hounding the police for months but they weren't telling her anything and it was so frustrating. It was as though her husband didn't even matter. Julia was now seeing for the first time in her life, something that she had never really thought about before; Julia was of the belief, that the police were not dealing with Joseph's murder the way they would, had he been white. She was now worried about the kind of experiences her daughters might face, and they wouldn't even have their father to help them understand life and the world as a person of colour. These were things that Julia had never considered before now. She'd never had reason to. It was a scary and uncertain future, that lay ahead for the four of them.

Kano. Julia had seen the lad's face around town, had recognised him when his photo was included in the very limited press coverage about his death; killed by two women, who were then, lawfully killed, by the police. That had been the conclusion, but by the time the gunfight and its casualties had been reported on, the crime scene was no longer a crime scene and the story had been spun, so that it was just some sort of love triangle, between the two female shooters and Shane; women that Shane had abandoned - with a child each - in London, over twelve years ago. The police hadn't had any choice but to shoot the armed women, and Kano's presence had remained unexplained and wasn't further investigated. Nobody seemed to think that there was any point. But Shane's death deserved more than that. He was worth a lot more than the other three reprobates, who were killed.

It had been a shock for Julia to learn that Shane had two teenage daughters, for women that were first cousins. That meant that Julia and Shane's three daughters, supposedly had two half sisters that were siblings and cousins at the same time. Julia had felt sick to her core; she really hadn't known her husband like she'd thought she had, but that didn't mean that she was going to stop loving him now, because of the posthumous revelations. Julia missed her man deeply, and her daughters wanted their dad back too. The police might need proof in order to pursue a prosecution but Julia did not need evidence to deliver her, justice for Shane. He would always be Shane to her. Joseph was not the man that she had married.

Julia kissed her three daughters good night - one kiss from her, and a second kiss from their dead father - and then turned out the bedroom light. Even though the girls had been sleeping in their own individual rooms, ever since they'd bought and moved into this bigger house more than three years ago, ever since Shane's death, all three girls had started sharing one bedroom again. Julia herself, found it difficult sleeping in her bed alone; reaching across to hug the love of her life and remembering that she would never be able to do that again. Not in this lifetime. Convinced that Shane's scent and pheromones were still everywhere in their bedroom, Julia had forbidden her cleaner to go in there for six months after Shane's death. No, Shane's murder.

She may be widowed, but Julia had plenty of money. Her family had always been well off, having owned a vineyard back home in France for almost a century, but now Julia had even more money. Money that Shane had earned, saved and invested through his hard work and risk taking. Work undertaken in order to be the best husband and father that he could possibly be. Shane had only been interested in loving and providing for his girls. Julia had known a better version of the man, whom was once known as Joseph. Both she and her daughters had had everything that they'd needed and wanted. Now Shane was gone. Forever. But Julia would love him eternally. Their vows didn't become exempt just because Shane had a past that was substandard. As long as she shall live, was the length of time that Julia would love her husband and seek retribution.

Of course she felt hurt and offended that Shane hadn't trusted her enough to be open and honest about his life in London, before they'd met - hiding the fact that he was already a father, was so not like the man that Julia had known and loved. Adored and cherished. She had struggled with the loss of Shane so much, that for a long while, Julia had doubted her ability to go on being a good mother, now that her other, better half was gone. But she was trying her best everyday, to be strong for their girls.

Resuming her position on the handmade Italian sofa in the living room, Julia stretched her couture trousered legs along the length of it. She'd spent plenty of time curled up with Shane, right here. Now her memories, were all that she had and Julia thought it was just so unfair. Unjust. With tears in her eyes, she kissed the photo of her late husband that was on the home screen of her iPhone 12 and vowed not to rest until Bradley Brown or someone very close to him, was dead. Dead just like the man she had believed, that she'd spend the rest of her life with. A life where, **mangez bien, riez souvent, aimez beaucoup**, had been their motto.

Julia opened up Facebook on her iPad and signed into the new fake profile that she'd made a few nights previously. Picking up her wine glass, she took a sip of Domaine Du Pélican. Julia didn't just drink her family's own wine; she was constantly trying other popular brands, to test the competition and she smiled now, at the fact that this particular wine, had nothing on their own pinot noir. Her smile widened farther when she spotted the new notification that she'd been waiting, hoping for. Through her teary eyes, she opened it up. A message informing her, that she was now friends with Candace Brown. She would befriend that bastards mother, and then she might slit her fucking throat and see how *le petit con* liked that. *Wayo*, as her husband would've said.

Julia Aku like Bradley Brown, also believed, that revenge had no expiration date and even if she had to wait another eighteen years for the man to be released from prison, she would get Bradley back. For taking their beloved husband and father away from them. That much was a given.

On récolte ce que l'on sèmee or as they say in English, What goes around, comes around...

About the Author

This is Jay's second self published work. After publishing her debut novel, *Caught In The Crossfire,* Jay decided that she also wanted to cater to a younger, more urban audience and for those who love reading but are put off by longer stories. Popular African, Caribbean and English proverbs are used to reflect the heritage, ethnicities and cultures of the characters in this novella because Jay feels that these are being lost in the generations that postdate the Millennials.

You can connect with me on:

https://www.jaywordauthor.com

Printed in Great Britain
by Amazon